ALSO BY PETE FANNING

Justice in a Bottle

Runaway Blues

Bricktown Boys

The Thing About Dad

Pete Fanning

IMMORTAL WORKS
Salt Lake City

Immortal Works LLC
1505 Glenrose Drive
Salt Lake City, Utah 84104
Tel: (385) 202-0116

Cover Art by Lenore Stutznegger
www.lenorestutz.com

ISBN 978-1-953491-42-8 (Paperback)
ASIN B0B41CY16Y (Kindle)

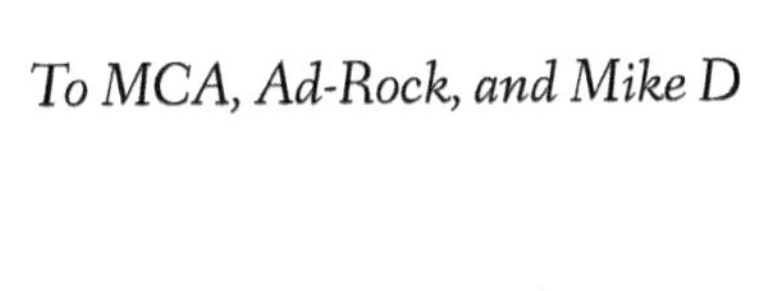

To MCA, Ad-Rock, and Mike D

It seemed like it all happened at once, the way an ordinary day became the turning point of my summer, maybe even my life. It was early June and Mom and I were out in the yard. Mom was watering the garden while I chucked my football into the maple tree, trying to free my glider from its branches. My grandfather had given the glider to me for my birthday last September, and it had been stuck up there ever since. The wind had done me no favors, so now, with only the tip of the wing poking out, the football was my only hope.

I cocked back for yet another wobbly heave when Dad's truck came barreling down the street. He honked, pumping his fist as the back tire hopped the curb and the truck lurched to a stop in the driveway. He sprang out without even bothering to shut the door.

"Well Marcus, we got it!" he announced, more dancing than walking. He tripped on the hose, and for a split second I thought Mom was going to drench him with it, but he caught himself, tipping right by her with a peck on the cheek before doubling back around like a baton twirler in a parade. "*The Bugle* came by today, they want to run a big story in the paper," he continued cheerfully.

I glanced at Mom, who sure enough had tightened her grip on the dripping nozzle. Another car rumbled down our street, a huge, whale of an antique I'd never seen before. "Welcome to the nineties, Newburg!" Dad belted to the clear blue sky.

What my dad meant was that after two years of rumors and gossip it was official—a Mega More super store was finally coming to Newburg. Eighty thousand square feet of retail bliss, it was enough to get even my dad to dance. He was slightly offbeat and out of tune but too worked up to care. I laughed too, not so much because I was happy about the store but because of how he was wailing like a loon out in the yard.

Only Mom wasn't laughing. Just the mere mention of Mega More and her lips curled into a mega snarl, usually followed by an epic rant about chain stores and corporate bullies. I'd learned from experience it was best to start nodding and backing out of the room when she got going. And if able, avoid the topic altogether.

Just last fall she'd gone before city council as the lone voice against the store, railing passionately about preserving history and trees and all that stuff minutes before the council voted 5-0 in favor of the "killer of culture" as she called it. But I don't think she had plans to give up, and it wasn't doing me any favors at school.

Dad came to his senses after the old clunker passed, more loud than fast and taking up every bit of the street. Mom let off the hose as she watched the rusty four-door float down the road, the back bumper nearly dragging because the car was packed to the gills with boxes and clothes and loose plastic bags fluttering out of the back windows. The car was so crammed with junk I couldn't even make out who was driving.

"Do you think someone's finally moving in?" I asked, seeing that the boat was pulling into the driveway at the old Ramsey place. It stopped with a bang, leaving a cloud of white smoke hanging like fog over the road. Mom coughed, waving her hand in front of her face even though the car was three houses away.

"Who knows," Dad said, squinting. "Wow, a sixty-three

Buick. I haven't seen one of those in a while. Maybe a sixty-four."

We stood on the lawn, all of us staring, as a boy around my age climbed from the car and started unloading boxes. It got my attention because, as it stood, I was the only kid on the street—if you didn't count Caitlyn Pettyjohn, my former babysitter who wished me dead.

I shielded the evening sun from my eyes, watching from the carport as the kid and maybe his dad opened the trunk and hauled boxes and lamps and other things into the house. Mom wiped the dirt from her hands and plopped down into her seat at the outdoor table. She already had the carport in full summer mode, after having Dad and me haul up all the pots for her plants and herbs along the ledge. The flowers spilled out of the hanging baskets.

"Well, maybe I'll make cookies to welcome them," Mom said. Dad and I exchanged glances. The only thing my mom's cookies shared with actual cookies was a name. For her last batch she'd used avocado instead of butter. They'd been hard enough to skip like stones across the creek.

"Let's just see what happens first," Dad said, still all jokes and smiles.

Mom hopped up to go check on dinner. I wondered how in the world this Mega More thing was going to work. For one, I never thought Dad's company would actually land the bid to clear the way for the store. And I don't think Mom did either, not while she spent her days writing to local officials or flooding *The Bugle* with editorials about the sanctity of our history. And now Dad was lacing up his boots to make a parking lot out of the rugged wilderness she wanted to wrap her arms around and protect.

Worst of all, I'd be caught in the middle of the mess. Normally I could deal with my mom's causes. She was out to rid the world of wrongdoing, and as far as I could tell there was no harm in that. She volunteered at the soup kitchen, organized fundraisers—she even collected coats for the needy during winter. Thanks to her, I'd spent more than a few Saturday mornings picking up trash on Route 43 without a coat to call my own. It was good for my soul, she'd say, reminding me about my civic duty to help those in need, even on the weekends. But the Mega More thing was different; looming like a meteor that was set to obliterate my summer, if not our house altogether.

After another fruitless half hour tossing the football at the glider and spying on the Ramsey place, Mom called me in for dinner. I swung through the door, rinsed my hands in the sink, then fell into my place at the table. Dinner. With all the talk of the store and the new neighbors, I never even saw it coming.

Fresh off the phone with work, Dad took his spot at the head of the table. Mom breezed into the dining room and set a blue rectangular dish on the flowery holder thing. I froze in my chair. Delicious things like hot dogs or pizza, even spaghetti, didn't arrive at our table in the blue dish. No, the blue dish meant only one thing.

"Meatloaf," Mom announced, lifting the lid with flourish, like a game show assistant.

She managed to say it with a smile. And even as she'd slathered the top with ketchup I knew what held that pulsing wet sponge of dinner together: carrots, red onions, asparagus, bell peppers, and the like. Calling it meatloaf should have been considered a criminal offense, because it wasn't "meat" at all, but a gathering of yuck.

Dad dug right in, too delirious to put up a fight. He wiped his face with his napkin and nodded my way, where a thick sludge of the stuff had found my plate. "Eat, Marcus."

I drew a breath and picked at it cautiously. It looked sort of like Aunt Joyce's fruitcake, and that wasn't helping things. Mom slid her chair closer to the table and narrowed her eyes at me. "Try it, Marcus."

Outnumbered, I managed a tiny bite. It wasn't too bad with all the ketchup escorting the way, but my relief quickly turned to horror when Mom plopped a spoonful of lima beans down beside the main course. My throat clicked as it tightened.

It's not that I didn't like vegetables. I could deal with green beans okay, especially if they were soaked in bacon first. Thing was, real bacon was about as rare as Leap Year in the Hawthorne household. Thanks to my mom I was probably the healthiest kid in the seventh grade. And thanks to her genetics, I was also one of the shortest. But tonight's meal was hardcore, even for her.

Instinctively, I leaned back from my plate. While the meatloaf threat had been neutralized by the ketchup, that small pile of lima beans had my eyes watering. Seeing the trouble I was having keeping things down, Mom issued a casual threat. "I can heat up the Brussel sprouts if you'd like."

Just that quickly, she bypassed all standard intimidation tactics and went straight for the nukes. Dad's head popped up, his smile slipping a notch as the big Buick lurched back up the street, eclipsing the evening sun and creating a much-needed distraction.

"Hopefully they'll be better than the last tenants," he sighed. Since the Ramseys had moved to assisted living, their old house had fallen apart. The wood siding was splintered, and the patchy roof was missing shingles. Dad could hardly look down the street without shaking his head at the long grass and the vines tangling up the azaleas. I seized the moment, using the opportunity to keep the conversation light and far away from Mega More, politics, and most importantly, those cruel and unusual lima beans on my plate.

"So Dad, who do you have in game two?"

We'd just watched Michael Jordan and the Chicago Bulls take it to Portland in game one of the NBA Finals, and I felt a sweep was coming. Dad turned away from the window.

"Come on, Marcus, the statistics show that the winner of game one wins the series sixty-seven percent of the time."

I nodded, edging some meatloaf over a lima bean, wondering if that was an actual stat or some number he'd plucked from his head. He did that sometimes, like when he told me that eighty-three percent of accidents on the job site were preventable. "What about the other seventeen percent?" I'd asked. He'd said that those were just accidents.

Mom cleared her throat. Dad's gaze fell to my plate. "Now eat your limas, Marcus," he said, ending any hopes I had of a veto. I forked two pellets, shivered, and washed them down with milk.

We survived dinner. I swallowed seven lima beans whole and Mom and Dad played nice, discussing summer plans and not the mega elephant in the room. I kept waiting for Mom to start up about the store, but she never did. And Dad was full of easy laughter and smiles. I figured that she was going to let him have his moment in the sun. But if Dad thought she would keep quiet about this, he was kidding himself. I knew better. I could see it in her eyes that there was major trouble ahead.

Later that night, while lying in bed, I felt a familiar clenching in my chest. I flipped and flopped, wondering how in the world Mom and Dad were going to keep from killing each other. When I got worked up my heart would skip beats and my mind would go spinning with possibilities. I took a deep breath. Dad liked to say that I could worry the shine off the moon. He'd told me to leave the worrying to him, that I was twelve and that I'd have plenty of things to worry about when I got older.

So I worried about that.

Waiting for the bus, I was hoping to get another glimpse at the new kid, but the windows at the old Ramsey place were dark and the place appeared dead to the world. The red Buick sat hulking in the driveway, where even the gentle morning sunrays didn't do it any favors. I tightened my grip on my backpack as the sound of grinding gears approached.

The therapy session was set to begin.

Being the first stop of the bus route, I began each school day by climbing aboard the empty vessel and directly into the fireball stare of Miss Mann. Miss Mann had driven buses for as long as there had been buses. I knew that because she'd told me several times. She had to be close to eighty, and she usually reeked of ripe perfume and cigarette smoke, yet no sooner than the doors shut and we got moving she'd let out a rasping hack and then launch right into her latest troubles with her lazy, stinking, good-for-nothing ex-husband.

Maybe I was easy to talk to, or maybe she thought of me as her personal shrink, a cheap and easy ear. Either way, I'd already tried sneaking back a row each morning until I found a spot near the back tires. But that only compelled her to take her eyes off the road so she could yell and cackle over her shoulder, which was more like what a wounded coyote might sound like in the wild. It was safer to move back up front.

Mr. Howell—my first period teacher—liked to say that we are the company we keep, and that's what I was thinking about at lunch as Danny Peebles—my sorta/kinda best friend—talked smack about how the Portland Trailblazers would take the Finals. Danny had moved to Newburg from Michigan in the third grade and we'd bonded over our love of sports. But these days it seemed to me like he picked against whatever I liked simply for the sake of arguing, and lately I'd found myself looking forward to summer for a break.

As far as the Finals, I wasn't so worried about Portland as I was that Mom would find out I'd managed to leave the house wearing a fraying, used-to-be-white-but-now-sort-of-gray Chicago Bulls cartoon-head t-shirt. I'd added a new jelly stain on Horace Grant's head to go with the crusty mustard stain on Scottie Pippin's nose. I'd managed to go undetected through breakfast, covering it with a collared shirt that I'd since ditched in my locker.

"You owe me a cookie crunch," I squeezed into the conversation when Danny finally stopped going on about how the refs were cheating. I wasn't a big-time gambler, but this was the Finals and we'd decided on a little wager for each game.

"Double or nothing?" he asked. His dark eyebrows arched, so badly wanting to touch. Sometimes they got their wish when he grimaced or was concentrating on a video game. I bit my lower lip. The way His Airness was playing I liked my chances.

"Deal," I said. "And Portland might want to play some defense. MJ hit six three pointers in the first half."

Danny rolled his eyes, took nearly half of his sandwich down, then cracked open a can of Pepsi. His dad drove a truck for Pepsi Cola and always had an endless supply of the stuff. He was always decked out with the latest merchandise, shirts and hats—he even had a Pepsi jacket. It was like his whole family was sponsored by soda.

The last week of school was practically pointless as far as learning went. The classroom was hot and all everyone talked about was summer vacation—Virginia Beach for most, although some went to Myrtle Beach or the Outer Banks. A few of the lucky ones went on big trips to Disneyland or Sea World and then came back with a bunch of blurry pictures of stuff you had to be there to appreciate. We hadn't discussed much about vacation at home because Dad was so worked up about Mega More, but I figured we'd at least go camping.

Hopping off the bus that afternoon, I quickly yanked on the collared shirt from my backpack. The sun barreled down on my back but was nothing compared to the heat I'd catch if Mom found out I'd worn my raggedy old good luck charm to school. Fixing my collar and wiping down the wrinkles, I spotted her out in the yard, digging in the flower bed. I crept down the driveway, tipping towards the carport when she popped up.

"Hey Marcus, how was school?" she asked, standing up and wiping her brow with her arm.

"Good, you know, regular old school and all." I picked up my pace. *Nope, nothing to see here,* I just needed to make it to the carport. Easy does it...

"Hey, come over here."

"Huh?" I stopped in my tracks. Mom was all over me, eyeing my neckline like a hawk. She could spot a speck of ketchup on my shirt from fifty yards away. And playing deaf didn't help, because she closed in on me with swift strides.

"Is that...?"

She lifted my collar and gasped. I hung my head in defeat.

"It's my good luck shirt, Mom."

"You wore that to school? Marcus Kennedy Hawthorne. Get in that house and put that shirt in the wash."

She loved to say my full name to add some extra salt to a scolding, but honestly, I think she just liked to hear it said out loud. As the story went, she and Dad had flipped a coin on who would get to pick my middle name. Mom chose heads. If it had landed on tails I would've been Marcus *Reagan* Hawthorne.

Thoroughly humiliated, I scooped up my book bag and limped inside. In the basement, I reluctantly tossed my beloved good luck charm into the dark abyss of the washing machine and then slunk off to my bedroom where I found a Nike t-shirt on the floor and gave it a whiff. Just under my feet, I heard the lid slam on the washer, followed by the menacing squeaks and swishes as the soap did its best to rid my shirt of its lucky powers.

Later, I found Mom in the kitchen chopping up basil, its sharp aroma reminding me that summer was near. She shook her head without turning around. I could tell she wasn't ready to let the shirt thing go. "You know, Marcus, I really wish you wouldn't sneak out of the house wearing filthy clothes."

"But Mom, it's the Finals."

She turned her head. "The what? Oh right, basketball. Okay, so maybe I'll buy a Bill Clinton shirt and wear it until the election, what do you think about that?"

I shrugged.

Politics were like sports for my mom. And with the presidential election being five months away, my parents were already locked into heated "discussions." Dad was a conservative and Mom was what he called a "bleeding-heart Liberal." I had no idea if that was a medical condition, but she seemed okay, even when she and Dad got into it and she'd purse her lips and grumble "Read My Lips" in a deep voice which never failed to send my dad into a tirade about taxes and Congress.

I thought they both needed help.

I woke up feeling sick. Last night, Dad and I watched in horror as the Bulls blew a ten-point lead in the fourth quarter only to cough up game two on their home court. Was it a mere coincidence that my good luck charm had been laundered and folded and was sitting neatly on top of the dryer? I didn't think so.

I plodded into the kitchen. Dad was reading the sports section at the table while Mom rinsed out a coffee mug at the sink. I fell into my chair at the table. She turned around with a smirk. "It's just a game, sweetie."

To Mom, sports were nothing more than a game played by overpaid Neanderthals. She didn't understand. I only half listened as she went on about how the teachers and social workers were the ones who should make the big bucks.

"The only problem there," Dad said, glancing up from the paper, "is that teachers and social workers don't pack paying customers into arenas or get television deals that make team owners money of which they use to pay the salaries of the front office, coaches, trainers and..."

Mom's glare cut him short, and he wisely took cover behind the sports section. I went for the Cheerios.

"Man, they sure did blow it in OT, didn't they?" Dad said as I came back to the table, stirring around my plain old oats in silence. I'd been lobbying for Honey Nut Cheerios, but every time Mom returned home from the grocery store, sure enough, it was that big canary-yellow box of un-honeyed, unsweetened cereal peeking out of her canvas bag.

Dad chuckled to himself. He was still riding high on the wave of the big story in *The Bugle*. He and his crew were going out to Squabble Creek today—the future site of Mega More. If everything went according to plan they'd be gearing up for their biggest job ever come fall.

Mom took a seat at the table, setting down her coffee mug with a spark in her eyes. "Did you read *all* of the paper?" she asked, or I should say, announced. Dad slowly lowered the newspaper. Mom lifted the mug to her lips, but her eyes were still doing plenty of smiling as she slid the local section toward him, folded over so the editorials faced up. In black bold print it read: *Mega More Offers No Local Value -Ana Hawthorne.*

Gulp. The paper fluttered under the gust of my dad's breath. Mom continued with the coffee. Her smiling eyes found me and she winked. I gulped again.

You would have thought that paper was solid steel the way Dad struggled to pick up that editorial. He gave it a thoughtful grimace, and then tossed the paper to the table. "Why, Ana? You know how big this opportunity is for us."

I started shoveling down cereal. My mom was a fantastic writer. She'd had a few columns published in various magazines and even an opinion piece in the *USA Today*. But like I said, what she enjoyed most was blitzing *The Bugle* with letters to the editor.

Now, setting her mug down, she tilted her head and cocked her eyebrows. Man, this was going to be a doozy. I knew from the thin smile on her lips she was ready for a bout. I'd looked through her old scrap books in the den, from her college years. She'd marched and protested just about everything: civil rights, women's rights, war, injustice, and police brutality. During one of her and Dad's skirmishes, I'd heard mention how she'd even been arrested. My mom, arrested!

Their eyes locked, and for a moment everything stopped as the house steeled itself for a clash. With only the newspaper between them, Mom set her hands around the coffee mug and smacked her lips. I could see her chewing at the inside of her cheek before she spoke, her voice controlled and steady. "Because Ben, some things are important. A sense of community. Local businesses. Have you seen what these stores do to communities—to local businesses?"

"Oh gee, I don't know," he shrugged. "Provide jobs, cut prices, help those in need?" Dad said, his great mood downshifting. I slurped the milk from my bowl, my eyes pinging from one parent to the other. Usually these debates were reserved for dinner, but Mega More had changed the game.

"*Help those in need?*" Mom scoffed. "Yeah, with those quality minimum wage jobs?"

Dad shook his head and rose to his feet. "I'm not doing this right now. I have to go to work, you know, to earn money, by building things. Like Mega More stores."

Mom shot Dad a look that could clean rust. No stranger to Mom's tactics, he managed to avoid her stare as he bent down and kissed the top of her head, his mouth parted like he had something else to say but then he thought better of it. Instead he turned to me. "Do you want a ride, Marcus?"

I sprang up, nearly knocking my chair to the floor. The chance to avoid Miss Mann and all her griping was like a surprise prison pardon. Mom closed her eyes and smiled.

In the truck, I could tell Dad was still thinking about that editorial. He checked the rear-view mirror, like he was worried he might still be within ear-shot of Mom. "You know, your mother means well, but she doesn't understand how the real world operates. She's stuck back in nineteen-seventy, burning bras and protesting Vietnam," he said, his big hands waving around the steering wheel.

I only nodded, because I didn't even know bras were flammable, and the more Dad went on the more I wondered just who he was trying to convince. Meanwhile I had my own worries. Like Danny and all the relentless heckling I was sure to receive. But when Dad flashed a playful grin and clicked his blinker as we neared McDonald's, I sat up straight and couldn't hide my smile.

"Now don't go telling your mother I'm letting you eat poison," he said. I shook my head vigorously. "This can be our little secret."

Fine by me. We pulled around to the drive-thru and I ordered a sausage, egg, and cheese biscuit. Dad got the same, but with a coffee.

Back on the road, Dad handed over my biscuit, which nearly fell out of my hands. Greasy goodness, I tore through it in five bites and then went for the cheese stuck to the wrapper. Dad looked over at me, his slate-blue eyes widening with surprise before he smiled at the pile of crumbs in my lap. We turned into Pleasant Day Middle School.

"All right, kiddo," he said, shaking my head playfully. "Have a good day, okay?"

I licked my lips, grabbed my bag, and slid out of the truck. "Thanks Dad."

On the first step I realized I was in serious trouble—much bigger trouble than Danny teasing me about the stupid game. My stomach bubbled, knocking me back a step. Something kinked and popped. I held my breath, hunched over beneath the tarmac. My intestines felt like they were in a knot, clogged and clicking like bad plumbing. Finally, with a slow, careful breath, I wiped my forehead and proceeded with caution.

I made it to my locker when Danny found me. "Well, how about those Bulls?" He smacked me on the back and my stomach gurgled.

"Old Air Jordan was grounded last night, huh?" he continued in his lisp, worsened by the wad of neon green gum flailing around between his chomping jaws. I winced, because my stomach kept grumbling like a pressure cooker.

"Whatever, they'll still win the series; it just won't be a sweep," I grunted.

"Well I guess we'll see about that."

The bell rang and everyone scattered like ants on a watermelon. I plodded toward Mr. Howell's class, my stomach having a tough time with the foreign contents. *What did they put in that stuff?* I thought, then silently cursed my mom because my poor stomach had not been vaccinated against the "poison of McDonalds" as she liked to call it.

As much as I hated public restrooms, there was no avoiding what had to be done. I sat through most of first period, sweating and wiggling until it was all I could do to get my hand up. I got a hall pass and crept down to the lower basin, past the gym and the machine shop and all the way to the quiet and deserted older part of the school. Less foot traffic meant fewer butts in toilet seats.

The first thing I did was kick the little door stopper and let the door swing shut. That way I thought someone might think the door was locked and move on. Then it was prep time. I scanned the stalls, where the doors were at one time white but now yellow with speckles of rust and stains.

All was clear. I chose the middle stall because everyone else chooses the farthest stall, thinking it was the least used. Rookie mistake. Inside my chamber, there was about half a roll of toilet paper, rippled like it had gotten wet and then dried, but there was no time. I stacked it high, lining the seat with layers. Then, after hearing only the occasional drip of the leaky faucet, I yanked my jeans down and hung on for dear life as I exorcised the demons.

Dad drove me over to Danny's house around four on Saturday afternoon. Even as we'd had our differences lately, traditions were hard to break. We'd been sleeping over at each other's houses for more than three years now, and Mr. Peebles was the coach of our baseball team. Not only that, Danny's house was always full of more junk food and soda than I could ever hope to consume. But that didn't mean I couldn't try.

Leaving our house, I spotted the new kid getting something from the trunk of the old car docked in the driveway down the street. He shut the trunk, saw me, and nodded his head. I nodded back as Dad backed out and got up the road.

At the Peebles' house, Danny opened the door, took one look at my Chicago Bulls lucky tee and rolled his eyes. "No Bulls fans allowed."

Mrs. Peebles peeked in from the kitchen, the cordless phone pressed against her cheek. Where my house sometimes got loud with debates and politics, the Peebles' house was noisy in a different way. TVs blared from every room, and Mrs. Peebles was constantly chatting on the phone. Danny's little brother Mikey was a mess, bouncing and screaming from his little chair as there was always some sort of mini crisis happening. Whenever I stayed with the Peebles, I came home exhausted.

I followed Danny to his room. The plan was movies, junk food, and video games, in whatever order. I wouldn't say there were no rules at the Peebles' house, but it was a totally different world from my household, where Mom and Dad were strict about dinners at the table, nightly showers, homework, and bedtimes.

Danny had two video game consoles, a Nintendo and the all new Sega Genesis. His stereo system had all sorts of cool lights on the equalizer with duel cassette and a CD player. On top of all that there was the nineteen-inch color television. His walls were covered with posters and pennants and all kinds of promotional stuff from Pepsi. A Pepsi clock, Pepsi stuffed animals, a dancing Pepsi can wearing shades, and a huge, *King of Pop* Michael Jackson Pepsi banner that spanned the wall near his desk.

After whipping me by two touchdowns in *Super Tecmo Bowl*, we trooped back to the kitchen to grab some snacks. Mrs. Peebles cackled into the phone. I tried to remember what she looked like without it stuck to her ear when Danny tossed me a soda. Oh boy.

I twisted the cap, igniting the spritz before I turned up a long, burning mouthful of Pepsi. Sweet Mother. I could practically feel my teeth rotting as the furious liquid sloshed around before scalding my throat. I had to stop and recover.

"You okay?" Danny asked between gulps. He'd nearly sucked down the entire bottle. Before I could answer, Coach Peebles bound into the kitchen and tore into the fridge. He too found a Pepsi, shut the door, then noticed me standing there, my tongue out, still trying to recover from the assault of the carbonation on my throat.

"Oh, hey Marcus."

"Hey Coach Peebles."

His gaze fell to my shirt. "Hey, you know you can't come in this house wearing that."

I glanced down at my shirt, then to Danny who smirked. "He's just kidding."

Coach Peebles, whose own shirt was grease-stained and filthy, steadied himself on the counter, his fingernails filled with dark crescents of grit. "Yeah, I'm only messing with you. But you might have to turn it inside out."

I could never tell whether Coach was teasing or not. He had those same accusing eyebrows as Danny, only with a goatee and dark eyes that came down on you like the bad guys in the movies. Whenever I struck out, which was a lot, he'd roll his eyes, sighing deeply until I came hobbling back to the dugout where he'd clap his hands and tell me it was all right, keep my head up. So I never knew what to make of it.

Danny and I stocked up on the Cool Ranch Doritos, Little Debbie's, Chips Ahoy, and even a bag of miniature Snickers bars—all akin to poison at my house. We hauled it back to his room, where we played video games until my hands hurt and my eyes were blurry. Mrs. Peebles ordered pizza, and it arrived as Danny and I surfaced from his room for more Pepsi.

With a plate of pizza, we all gathered around the big screen television. Coach Peebles had rented *Terminator 2* from the video store. And they had one of those projection screens with big speakers that felt like the movie theater and rattled the just-a-little-too-life-like statue of Jesus on the crucifix mounted on the wall.

Danny and I settled in with pillows on the floor. My stomach was reeling after the onslaught of sugar I'd poured into it. I knew Mom would never let me over again if she knew what I was eating, drinking, or watching, but I managed to push those thoughts aside. At least until Coach Peebles called me out again.

"Hey Marcus, I read your mom's letter to the editor. What's she got against Mega More?"

"Huh?"

Suddenly all the Peebles—even Mikey—were looking at me. I squirmed from my spot on the floor. "Oh, uh, I don't know."

Coach Peebles shook his head, a giant slice of double pepperoni dangling from his hand. "I mean, I can't wait for Mega More to get here. I'll be able to go to one place and get everything I need. Besides, Carol might apply for a job there," he said, nodding to Mrs. Peebles who may or may not have heard him with the phone and all. "They pay pretty good, right Carol?"

Mrs. Peebles nodded. I wasn't sure what I was supposed to say to all this. But here they were feeding me pizza and soda, and so I felt obligated to sit, half turned away from the television, sort of twisted around to listen.

He took down a bite of pizza, wiped his chin. "And didn't your dad get the bid? At the site?" he scoffed. "She's going to make trouble for him, that's for sure."

Still turned around, I tried to think of something meaningful to say. I hadn't thought about everyone in town reading Mom's stupid letter to the editor. Now I wondered if she hadn't thought about making my life miserable, but I was sure going to tell her. Thankfully, Danny finally came to my rescue.

"Well, Marcus didn't write it, Dad."

Coach Peebles set his pizza on his plate. He reached for his soda. "Ah, Marcus knows I'm just giving him a hard time," he said, his dark eyes squinting with his smile. Then he looked to me again. "But do me a favor. Tell your mom this town wants a Mega More."

5

Take a few spots of Pepsi, a couple quarter-sized splotches of pizza sauce, a light dusting of cheese ball powder, and back-to-back ninety-degree days, and what do you have? A fully restored good luck t-shirt.

The Bulls got back on track Sunday afternoon, taking what the announcers called a commanding 2-1 lead, and I was able to show my face at school again on Monday to collect my cookie crunch. Victory was delicious.

After school I managed to slip inside and change t-shirts without drawing attention. In the kitchen, I poured a glass of Tang—which tasted tart and terrible after a weekend sucking down soda—but it wasn't the ice-cold Tang that sent shivers down my back. No, it was the electronic sound of keys, more specifically, Mom on her IBM Wheelwriter.

I tipped toward the den, the ice cubes rattling against my glass as I peeked in and found Mom at her desk, click-clacking away. Whatever she was hacking out was sure to spell trouble for me. Remembering the interrogation over at the Peebles' on Saturday, I'd worried myself into a puddle in bed last night, imagining more angry mobs showing up in our yard with torches and sticks, this time demanding Mom be stopped or jailed for writing such inflammatory things about Mega More.

Extreme? Maybe. But if she kept this up, I was going to get tagged as the kid with the weird mom. Pretty much the same thing. I started worrying about that so much I didn't even notice the clacking had stopped.

"Marcus?"

"Mom, please. No more letters," I said, sliding off the doorjamb into the room. She lifted her glasses, looking up from her typewriter.

"Well hi to you too, sweetie. How was your day?"

"Good. It was fine." I glanced over her shoulder. "What are you writing?" I said, motioning to the typewriter. She raised an eyebrow, surprised or amused by my question, which sounded more like an accusation.

"I'm writing to our congressman. Is that okay with you?" she asked, and then her eyes fell to my chest. "That shirt, Marcus, ugh."

I glanced down to find I already had stains on the replacement shirt. No time to worry about with that, though. *Congressman*. Yikes. I had to put a stop to this. Yet, sure enough, as I took down another sour sip of Tang, smacking my lips and trying to stay focused, Mom turned and started banging on the keys again.

"Mom, a lot of people don't think you should be writing those...letters."

The words were gone before I could get them back. But I had her attention. The typing came to an abrupt halt, and she turned around with a smile curling up her lips. "They don't? Do these people include, say, Jerry Peebles?"

Jerry. Coach. Man, she'd put that together in a hurry. I took a breath. Things were off to a rough start. Always a bad tactic, telling my mother someone didn't like what she was doing. It was like daring her to wallpaper the town with letters. My mind flooded with fear, my thoughts turned to mush. All I had was volume, so I raised my voice to match the increasing panic in my head. "What's so bad about Mega More? People will get jobs and cheap prices."

My mom calmly adjusted the paper in her Wheelwriter. She lifted her glasses, carefully setting them on the table. When she swung her legs around from the chair and tucked her chin onto her arms resting on the top of the chair—like she was fascinated with whatever I had to say—I knew I was in trouble. "Go on—jobs, cheap stuff..."

I tried to arrange the cluttered thoughts in my head. "Well it's just, people are excited about the store, and you're, I don't know, trying to ruin it."

My mom thought about this for maybe two seconds before she sat up straighter and took a deep breath. "Marcus, what do you think about a little field trip?"

"Uh, what do—"

"Come on, just the two of us." She stood and launched into one of her little yoga stretches. She set a hand on my back. "I'd like to show you something."

Mom's car was in the shop, where it could be found more often than our driveway. So she suggested we take our bikes— hers with a hideous basket and bell on the handlebars and me on my BMX I'd gotten two years ago. My knees always hit the handlebars when I pedaled hard. I kept forgetting to ask Dad to raise them.

We drifted down Maple Run then cut over to Wilson Road, crossing at the light where we rode on the sidewalk past the Drug Fair pharmacy and the gas station. If there was anything worse than seeing your mom pedaling her bike around town—using hand signals, no less—it was riding around *with* her and being a part of the dorkiness. At first I tried turning my head away from traffic the best I could, hoping not to be recognized, until I nearly ran off the road.

Things were better on Squabble Creek Road. There was

less traffic, and we cruised along, beneath an old bridge then under a canopy of enormous Sycamore trees. Things got bumpy as the road was paved but rutted, gravelly with dirt-worn ditches around the bends. A few pickup trucks putted past us, the only reminder that we weren't in the wilderness.

Mom slowed, drifting casually around the bend until the road straightened. A sagging wooden fence struggled to contain a field of wildflowers and tall grass. I followed her wobbly turn down a dusty path where I caught up to her side.

"Some field trip, Mom. We should come here this summer instead of the beach."

"Right up here," she said, ignoring my sarcasm. The path sloped and wound until we arrived at an enormous chestnut tree. Its thick, low-hanging limbs spread wide like a hand ready to catch a ball from the sky, and its knobby roots elbowed out of the ground, worn and smooth as old furniture.

Mom smiled, pointing to a splintered sign hanging from a wrought iron pole.

Squabble Creek Cemetery

I'd been fishing with Dad here before. I recognized the remains of an ancient water mill near the embankment. But we always came at the crack of dawn, so I wasn't exactly observing my surroundings. In fact, I didn't even know the cemetery was back there until Mom motioned to the old grave markers spread over the hill nearly overgrown with brush.

The small creek gurgled over the rocks. A wall of oaks and sycamore trees stood as a backdrop. Mom parked her bike at the sprawling chestnut, even putting an arm around it.

"This tree is more than one hundred years old, Marcus."

"Mom, you're literally hugging a tree."

"Come on, let's take a walk." We left our bikes at the tree. "This cemetery holds the history of our town. Listen."

Listen? Were the dead bodies going to speak to us? I cocked my head, only catching a faint swoosh of traffic up on Wilson, some birds chirping, crows cawing. Not much else going on. "Okay?"

It was no use. Mom was off in La La Land. I slogged behind her as we ambled along between old headstones and monuments. "There are soldiers buried here, sheriffs and local politicians." She motioned past a felled tree over to some rocks and weeds. She pointed out where the confederate soldiers were buried, then to the much smaller slave cemetery. She shook her head with a frown, said something about how people were segregated even in death.

I followed her gaze toward the field in the distance. Mom closed her eyes, craning her neck as though the wind was speaking to her. Then we rambled on, past a row of old dogwoods where some stone markers peeked out of the grass, stopping at a tiny clapboard chapel. From a distance I'd thought it was gray, but as we got closer it was just old and worn.

"This is one of the oldest cemeteries in the state."

Most of the headstones were jagged and chipped, the names so washed out of the stone I couldn't make them out. I jumped as a horn bellowed, some chugging before a train cut through the wilderness, its railcars screeching on the other side of the oaks. We watched until it was gone. In its wake, the cemetery seemed even quieter than before.

I looked up to Mom. "Okay, so what's with the history lesson?"

"Well, now look over there, past the fence back toward that beautiful tree."

I followed her finger back to our bikes, then to a sagging

split-rail fence on the other side of the gravel road and back to the chestnut tree.

"Yeah?"

She shrugged. "Well, that's where the Mega More is going."

I glanced back at Mom. She was still an inch or so taller than me. I was hoping to get that growth spurt this summer and finally overtake her. "Wait," I said, looking back and forth. I was surprised at how far we'd walked. I pointed back, just to be sure. "Right there?" She nodded. "But how are they going to fit it there?"

"Oh, they will. They'll move the creek, grade the land, widen the road, and tear down that inconvenient old structure and build it." Another shrug.

"*Move* the creek?"

"Divert. Move. Oh, and the parking lot will be marvelous, it should make it all the way up to our bikes, probably. Because you have to put all of those shoppers' cars somewhere."

Mom was pretty good at the sarcasm, too. And even though I knew she was being dramatic, at least I hoped so, my lungs expanded as I took in the tranquility surrounding us. I imagined all the traffic pulling in and out at all hours, the litter on Wilson Road strewn across the sleepy cemetery. The shopping carts, the big bright lights, and pavement over the dusty stones, the noise of the construction. Dad's construction.

"Why would they put it here?"

She wiped at her shirt. "Why not? The land is cheap, there's lots of space. A nice, big open field to pave. We're right off the main road, Marcus. They have ambitious plans for this area, Lower Wilson Road, as they're already calling it. Soon there will be condos, restaurants, shopping..."

My neck and shoulders rippled with a chill. Mom smiled knowingly, as though reading my thoughts. "Starting to see why I write those pesky letters to the editor?"

I nodded before I could think. As though to prove Mom's point, a hawk flew over us, wings outstretched as he cut through the air toward a tree limb. "But I mean, they won't actually pave *over* the cemetery, right? Dad said they'd pay to have it re-fenced, right?"

She scoffed. "Oh sure, and who doesn't love a tourist attraction beside a Mega More? They should put one at Yosemite too, don't you think?"

"Mom, this isn't Yosemite," I said, coming to my senses. But there was no arguing with her on this. Dad had surely tried. Although being out there with her right then, with that hawk and the small glittering creek, the massive chestnut tree, it was hard to argue against what she was saying. "Why not do it up there on Wilson Road?"

Mom put a hand on my shoulder. "Exactly. Everyone thinks I'm against Mega More, which might be partly true, but my fight is for this spot right here," she said, tapping up dust with her foot. "Once it's rezoned, that's it. It's over."

We walked along the headstones, the sun on our backs and our thoughts with the dead. I was kind of mixed up, because what did I know about zoning? And people did need jobs and affordable groceries, but every time I looked back at that old chapel, all I saw were tractors and bulldozers and the dirt and dust of construction. Mom kept her hand around my shoulders, which was fine with me. Nobody came down Old Squabble Creek Road.

Not yet anyway.

Welcome to the Hawthorne dinner table. Tonight's debate will take place over a main course of wheat pasta with Spinach Florentine sauce and homemade rolls, complimented by a leafy side-salad with balsamic vinaigrette. This evening's topic will be the Mega More store, the one my father is building and my mother is protesting.

Let's begin, shall we?

Things began innocently enough, with Dad and I discussing the Bulls' chances in the series. I figured they'd win out, like they did with the Lakers last year, but Dad thought Portland had shown some fight and could make things interesting—kind of like dinner got interesting once he took a bite of his roll and said, "Hey, what's up with the bikes out front, you two go for a ride?"

I shot a glance Mom's way, betrayal sitting heavy as a brick in my stomach. A quick sip of water and she wiped her mouth, where I couldn't be sure, but it looked like a tiny smirk had formed. "We did. Marcus and I took a trip to Squabble Creek Cemetery."

Gulp.

Dad took it in stride, or, with a nod, chewing for what seemed like a few years before tossing out the opening jab. "Well good, now you'll know how to get out to the Mega More store when we get it built."

I twirled the noodle onto my fork until the sauce dripped onto the edge of the table. I managed to wipe it up before it hit my lap, then I peeked up to Mom, whose smirk was still in place but her eyes had narrowed, catching a sharp gleam of the evening sun.

"Well, I thought it would be good for Marcus to see some of our town's history, at least before it's bulldozed to rubble."

"No one is *bulldozing* the cemetery, you know that."

"They might as well be, but you know, people need their parking and cheap plastic products more than they need history, right?"

"You've got to be kidding me, Ana. The store will be over two hundred yards away."

"Until they realize all of those shoppers will be famished, what they need is a burger joint next to the Mega More, because, well, you can sure work up an appetite from strolling those long aisles, and since the zoning has changed, why not toss in a video store, and maybe a multiplex while we're at it."

"Sounds like progress," Dad said, turning to me. "Marcus, does that sound like a bad deal to you? Burgers and movies?"

I spooned some more sauce into my noodles. Burgers and movies sounded great, of course. But then I thought back to the cemetery. "Yeah, but why can't they put the store up on Wilson Road? Why do they need a *Lower* Wilson Road?" I asked before my brain had a chance to screen the question.

My parents stared at me, Mom with pride and Dad with shock. I squirmed in my seat, my gaze falling to my plate where I'd poured way too much sauce and my noodles were drowning. My shirt (not my good luck charm) was splattered with buttery droplets of sauce and cheese.

The whole thing reminded me of Social Studies, when Mr. Howell had us pick a country and write a two-page paper about its people and culture along with its economic system, government, resources, and so on. Everyone wanted the United States, with England, Italy, and France being the next picks. But only one student could do a country. With a spin of the globe, I got Switzerland. And what I liked best was a little thing called Swiss Neutrality.

Now, under the intense heat of Dad's glare, I longed for such neutrality. Because in this little country of Hawthornia, where there is an ongoing struggle for power in its two-party system, it was the common folk like me who paid the price as Mom and Dad clashed over nightly battles about which system worked best.

Dad shook his head. "It isn't my job to decide where to put the store. It's my job to help build it. And if they do develop the land, that means more work for me, more jobs for the town."

Mom shook her head. "But you know it's not right to develop that land. It's sacred ground."

"It's called a job, Ana, and if a movie theater or burger shop comes to town, people have to work there." He threw up his hands. "Everyone wins.

"Oh yes, trickle down, right. Seems to me like the CEO of Mega More is winning more than the cashiers. These jobs you speak of, they're all rock bottom wages."

The Mega More debate took a turn and branched off toward Ronald Reagan, touching on Bush before inevitably arriving at the upcoming election. As they went on, I thought more about the warring factions of Hawthornia.

Hawthornia's small economy struggled with the ups and downs of the market. I decided that Hawthornia's biggest import was milk, and its biggest export was Mom's homemade salsa. Hawthornia's gross domestic product? Definitely lima beans.

Thinking about that made me squirt our biggest import out of my nose.

"Do you need a bib, sweetie?" Mom asked. Dad was looking at me like I was crazy.

"What? Oh, no. I'm okay."

And just like that, Mom and Dad's debate was forced to a draw as they took turns joking and laughing at my expense.

I saw it both ways. Sure, the town was growing and a Mega More would bring jobs with it, but then again, why did it have to be built at Squabble Creek? Mom was right, it wouldn't stop there, soon that cemetery would be sandwiched in between a gas station and a strip mall, and eventually everything would get bulldozed.

I tossed and turned over it in bed, thinking about my trip with Mom. Sure, Mom embarrassed me with her riding around town and her crusade against Mega More, but she was only doing what she thought was right. And so was Dad. He was bringing home a paycheck to put food on the table, which he thought was right.

Thing was, if they were both right, who was wrong?

Despite the impressive collection of colorful stains on my t-shirt, the Blazers managed to even up the series before the last day of school. But all wasn't lost, being the last day, I scored another ride with Dad. And another biscuit. My stomach must have been prepared because it only grumbled a little before it settled down without me having to snag a hall pass.

I was cleaning out my locker before lunch when Danny came bouncing down the hall. I took a breath, preparing for the inevitable, but he didn't even mention the game.

"So your mom is still writing those letters, huh?"

"I guess."

His caterpillar eyebrows had a face-to-face meeting on his head. "What's her deal, man?" He leaned against the locker beside mine. "Who doesn't like Mega More?"

I shut my locker and took a deep breath. In a way, this conversation was worse than the heckling. "I don't think she's really against the Mega More, but where they want to build it." I left out the part that if he'd actually read her editorial he'd know that. As far as I knew, Danny only read the back of video games, and I think he only skimmed those.

He knocked his head back with a laugh. "What, on some cow pasture?"

"Have you been down there recently?"

"Nope. Why?"

"There's a cemetery, with a chapel. An old graveyard, like, hundreds of years old. And this big chestnut tree, it's—"

"Really?"

"Yeah."

He seemed to be mulling it over, until he pushed off the locker, dancing around and wiggling his fingers. "A graveyard. Ooh, a haunted Mega More store! Like Poltergeist or something!"

I grabbed my book bag. What was the point? "Let's go to lunch."

"Yeah, you owe me a cookie crunch."

The last day of school ended exactly like last year. We filed into the cafeteria, where like last year it had been transformed into an auditorium. And then again, like last year, Principal Wiggins trotted out on stage as *"Ice Ice Baby"* thumped over the speakers.

Our principal's attempts at being cool usually fell as flat as the comb-over on his head. From the fist-pumping to the head-bobbing, the botched slang and outdated dance moves, we sat there in a collective cringe as he quoted Wayne's World. His send-off was also the exact same speech he'd given at the end of sixth grade. Right down to the "You don't know what you can achieve until you spread your wings and fly."

Personally, I was glad to put the seventh grade behind me. It had been memorable, but not in a great way. For one, I'd gone out for the track team back in the spring. Well, maybe not "gone out" because the track team doesn't exactly cut anyone. But I'd wanted to play a school sport, and being that I'm too scrawny for football and too slow for basketball, track seemed like the perfect way to at least be a part of something. Thing was, that something ended up being running lung-sucking circles around the track every day after school from March through May.

Coming home I had a summer-is-here skip to my step. The

sun was a little brighter and the trees a little greener. Even Hannibal, Ms. Tinkerton's menacing guard dog, seemed okay, watching me from inside the screen window.

I breezed down the street, ready to sling my book bag into my closet and shed my pants for shorts, when I found Mom kneeling behind her little car parked in the driveway. Relief washed over me. Good, no more biking around town. And I couldn't help but laugh as she smoothed down the bright blue *Clinton/Gore* '92 sticker she'd slapped over the *Dukakis/Bentsen* '88 sticker, beside the sun faded, *Buy Local* sticker that was peeling around the edges.

"You got your car back?"

She stood and admired her handiwork. "Yep, your dad worked something out with the garage."

"Well, he's going to love that," I said, nodding to the sticker. He'd spent the past four years making fun of the Dukakis sticker. Mom smiled, putting her arm around me.

"So how was it, kiddo?"

"We got the spread-your-wings-and-fly speech again."

"What?"

"Nothing. It was great. Hey, did you write another editorial today?"

She gave me a quick smirk. "Well, actually, I sold a piece to Millwright Magazine."

"Really, the one you've been excited about? That's pretty cool."

"Yeah, wait until I tell your father," she said, her eyes dancing. I chuckled, because they seemed to enjoy their political duel. Had they always been this way? We started toward the house.

"So you and Dad met when you were in college, right?"

"Yep. My junior year," Mom said with a laugh. "He and some friends lived a few houses up from my apartment."

I nodded. "Did you guys always, uh, disagree on things."

She closed her eyes. "Well, for the most part, yes. Even back then we were political opposites. In fact, the night we met, he and his friends came over and we got into this huge argument over the Vietnam War. By the time he left, I vowed that I'd never see him again."

"But obviously you did."

"Well, he's awfully cute, you know."

"Gross."

Mom laughed, squeezing my shoulder. "But that's the thing about your father, even though we don't see the political world the same way, he is thoughtful and caring and you might not know this, but he's very romantic."

I held up my arms in surrender. "Okay, sorry I asked."

"He's funny too. You know, besides his boneheaded political views, he's nearly perfect." She shot me a wink. "But give me some time. I'll wear him down."

———

A WEEK later the Chicago Bulls took the NBA Finals and I let Danny hear all about it for the entire two-hour bus trip to Wildwood Lake, where we spent the next five days hiking, camping, fishing, swimming and otherwise getting riddled with mosquito bites. Every year we looked forward to summer camp, and every year on the bus ride home, we couldn't wait to return to warm showers and cable TV as we clawed at our whelps and bites and vowed never to return.

Unlike school, summer was already flying away. June was scorching along; July was right around the corner. And that meant we were one month closer to the upcoming presidential election, and, like a bullseye on the calendar, the Mega More ground-breaking ceremony.

U nder the delusion she could stop a giant retailer promising the most convenient shopping experience under the sun, my mom rolled up her sleeves and started a petition to halt construction of the Mega More store. Through sheer grit and determination, she gathered maybe fifty or so signatures—impressive considering I couldn't think of a single soul who didn't want a new store in town.

Dad called it "cute." But cute was not the word I was thinking, not after Danny had ragged on me every day at camp, asking if my mom was going to live in a tree over at Squabble Creek. I laughed it off, at the same time hoping Mom never thought of that herself.

For me though, it was nice to sleep in, think less, and bask in the laziness of a hot summer day. And it was on one of those lazy days of doing nothing that I dusted off my skateboard and took to the street.

It was slow going, I was rusty and never that good to begin with. And I rode goofy-footed, meaning right foot first. Anyway, I was putting around like that when the new kid stepped out onto the front stoop. He watched me for a minute before his face brightened and he hopped of the porch and started toward the street.

"Aw snap! Is that a Vision Gator?"

Snap? The board wobbled and I bailed, stumbling off before I hit a car or face-planted into a telephone pole. Again,

I wasn't much of a skater. I ran down to catch the runaway skateboard my dad had found at a yard sale a while back. I picked it up and turned it over to the crazy lines that reminded me of a Dr. Suess book. Sure enough, it read "Gator."

I nodded. "Um, yeah," I said, setting it back down on the street.

"What's up man, I'm Cullen." He stepped closer to inspect my skateboard. He had one of those chain wallet things, the chain dangling from the back pocket to the belt loop of his unevenly cut-off shorts. "You live up there, right?" he said, looking up and pointing to my house. I nodded again, trying to keep up with his intensity.

"Yeah."

"Hey, do you mind?" he asked, nodding to the skateboard. I pushed it to him with my foot and he kicked up the tail and snatched it with his other hand. I'd tried that before, only to have the nose hit me in what Dad referred to as my wedding tackle.

Cullen hopped on the skateboard like it was nothing, the wallet chain bouncing with his jaunty pace. He tore down the street where he kicked the tail. The board shot into the air and flipped over a few times before he landed, the wheels slapping asphalt as he kept rolling. It was something I'd only seen on TV.

"Whoa."

He pushed along on the street, fast and easy, his body twisted slightly to the side, crouching as he kicked and flipped the skateboard again under his feet in one fluid motion. He wiped back his bangs, then spun around and tore back up the street for me. I was about to jump out of the way when he leaped off and tipped the skateboard up and handed it to me.

"Thanks, it's been a while since I've been on a board."

I took my old "board," which felt different in my hands, as

though it had been holding all sorts of secrets while sitting in our musty basement. "So, uh, where are you from?" I asked.

"From parts unknown," he said in a weird voice, waving his arms around. I must have been staring at him like he was an alien because he laughed. "I'm messing with you. We drove up from Florida," he said, his gaze falling to the skateboard.

"Are you uh, going to Pleasant View next year?" I asked, thinking I'd finally have someone other than Mrs. Mann to talk to on the bus. I figured he would be in middle school. He didn't look too much older than me, with his narrow shoulders and jagged hair, he was nearly as scrawny as me and only a hair taller. His knees and elbows were spotted with nicks and scabs in various stages of healing. He was kind of a mess, yet carried himself with a kind of coolness I could never grasp.

"Is that the name of the school?" He laughed. "Wow. *Pleasant View*," he said in a funny voice, nodding his head and planting a fist on his hip with a goofy smile.

I'd never given the name much thought. But now, hearing Cullen say it, I guess it was kind of a goofy name. We stood in front of his house, where the hood was up on the Buick. "My dad likes your car," I said, because I couldn't think of anything else.

He shot me a smile. "The beater?"

Just then a loud bang erupted from inside the house. Cullen turned back to me. "So check it, I gotta run. Maybe we can hang sometime."

"Yeah, um, sure."

"Cool. Later, man."

"Uh, later."

He took off, hopping the steps as he rushed inside. The screen door slammed shut and he was gone.

I spent the rest of that afternoon trying to get that skateboard off the ground while at the same time saying things like, "check it", and "aw snap", to myself. All I got for my efforts was a big old bruise on my right thigh.

Dinner was a chicken Caesar salad, one of Mom's favorites. Dad and I had enough sense not to complain. Also not discussed was the Democratic Convention, only days away, or how Dad had countered Mom's bumper sticker with his own shiny *Bush/Quale '92* sticker. But there was still plenty of time for politics to be addressed. After all, the election itself was still four months away.

Things were heating up on the local front, too. Dad and his crew were finishing up a couple of small jobs before the big dig over at you-know-where for you-know-what. Meanwhile, Mom planned to address city council next week. They might have been playing nice for now, as the two sworn enemies sat down, cordially passing croutons, but I knew it wouldn't last.

"I met the neighbor kid today," I said, munching on a crunchy piece of romaine lettuce. *No wonder my rib cage looks like an actual cage*, I thought, pushing the leaves around and hunting for chicken. I'd been eating rabbit food and tofu all my life.

Mom tilted her head. "Oh?"

"Yeah, his name is Cullen. He's going to be an eighth grader next year too. I think."

Dad nodded. "Well, good, it'll be nice to have some more kids on this street."

"Well, there's Caitlyn," I said, feeling a wave of red roll over my face.

Dad gave me a sharp look. "Don't get me started."

"Anyway, I think he's a skateboarder. He showed me a few tricks."

Mom looked up from her bowl. "Tricks? Oh, Marcus. Please tell me you wore your helmet."

Dad scoffed. "Helmet? When I was his age, I once jumped

off my dad's Olds on my bike." He tapped the side of his head. "Landed right on my noggin, and you know what? I got up, shook it off, and tried it again."

Mom shot me a wink. "Explains a lot."

***

THE NEXT DAY I found my helmet sitting on the kitchen table. I couldn't imagine wearing it around Cullen so I stashed it in my room and set off for Cullen's house on foot. When I got there, he was pumping up the tires on an old bike. He asked if I wanted to go exploring. I didn't tell him I'd already explored everything— having grown up in Newburg I knew every trail and shortcut. Besides, it wasn't like I had other plans. I said "sure" and ran up to grab my bike.

We rode through the woods to the park. Taking another look, I recognized the makings of Cullen's bike, parts of it, at least. The blue frame with a few scabs of rust had belonged to one of old man Ramsey's grandkids—it had sat abandoned against the house in the backyard for at least a few years. The black handlebars were missing grips, and the tires—one bigger than the other—were a little dry-rotted. Not that it mattered, Cullen could do as many tricks on that hunk of junk as the skateboard—bunny hopping the curb and riding wheelies for ten, twenty feet at a time.

We hit the park, circled around, and headed back the way we'd come. As we rode the trail, I took in his clothes. Where Danny always had the latest trends, the newest Reebok's or Nike Cross-trainers to match his outfits, Cullen didn't seem to care at all. With his frayed and stained khaki shorts and neon tank top, his style was all his own. As we rode into the haze of summer, his worn, checkerboard Vans became a blur as he pedaled, and it was all I could do to keep up.

When we got back to our street, Cullen set his bike by the old Buick and quickly turned for the front porch. "Well, that was fun, man. I gotta jet."

Jet. I added it to my growing vocabulary as I searched the streaked windows of the Ramsey house. Only a few boxes in the sill, but otherwise blank and dark. Cullen was already at the door when I yelled out, "Okay, uh, cool. See you tomorrow then?"

Cullen shrugged. "Bet."

Cullen and I hung out most of the week, either at my house, on the street, or at the park. Mom took to Cullen right away, the easy going way about him, how everything was cool or awesome, rad or chill. When she asked about his parents, he shrugged and said his dad was fixing the house up for reduced rent while looking for work.

On most days, around ten or so, I'd drift down the street in front of his house until he came out. Then he started showing up at my house. Like on Thursday, when I heard him around ten or so, singing and dancing on the carport as I opened the door.

"So watcha, watcha, watcha want?"

I looked around, confused. "What do *I* want?"

Cullen laughed. "You know, the Beastie Boys?"

I had no clue what he was talking about. Plus, I was a little embarrassed because I was wearing the baggy, Teenage Mutant Ninja Turtles t-shirt I always slept in.

Shaking his head, he smacked me on the back, brushing past me into the kitchen. "We'll get you straight. So what's up for today?"

I shrugged. Cullen slid his headphones from his ears to his neck, the cord tucked into the collar of his Red-Hot Chili Peppers tee, exiting at the bottom where it met the Walkman clipped to his waist. "Um, we could ride bikes to the park?"

He bobbed his head. "That's cool."

As usual, Mom was busy pounding away on the keys in the den, most likely firing off another tirade to *The Bugle*. I peeked in to let her know we were hitting the trails on our bikes.

Cullen craned his neck. "So what's your mom writing in there?"

I guided him back to the carport. I didn't need him to see how big of a dork my mom was. "Oh man, you don't want to know."

"Yeah I do."

"Hang on."

I changed clothes and we grabbed our bikes. Hannibal spazzed from his place across the street, yapping wildly, about to tear through the screen. Cullen asked again about what Mom was writing. I shrugged. I didn't feel like defending her again.

"Well, you've probably heard about the Mega More they're supposed to be building here next month."

Cullen shook his head. "Nope, I don't really keep up with the news."

"Oh, well, anyway, they're building it over on Squabble Creek Road, near the cemetery. My mom is trying to stop it."

"Stop it?" he said with a grin. "Like, how?"

We started down the street, hopping the curb at Caitlyn's house to the trail that cut through to the park. I explained everything to Cullen, about Mom's battle with the city council, the planning commission, and even the whole thing with Dad and the construction. By the time I was done blabbing we were halfway to the second bridge at the park, nearly two miles from my house, give or take.

We stopped at the creek, watching the dragonflies skim across the water, leaving rings that reminded me of a sonar screen. Surprisingly, Cullen didn't start in about Mom, about how the town *needed* a Mega More. He picked up a rock and skimmed it half a mile down the water.

"Man, that sounds like a tough spot. It's your dad's job to build your mom's nemesis."

"Her *what*?"

Cullen tossed a rock into the creek, causing the flies to scatter. "Her sworn enemy. The Mega More."

He made it sound like *Star Wars* or something. But hey, it was better than how Danny teased me about it. I picked up a rock. "Oh, yeah. I know, and they argue about it all the time. That and the election."

"It's all politics." He shrugged.

"Yeah, don't get them started on that." I tried to skim my rock across the creek, but it shot into the water with a *plunk*.

"Well, at least they care enough to vote," Cullen said, sort of under his breath.

"What do you mean?"

He side armed a stone and it skipped five or six times, clear across the creek. "My dad doesn't really do the voting thing," he said with a smirk.

These words were akin to treason to my mom. I threw another stone. *Plunk*. "Why not?"

Cullen grinned, kicked at the rocks. "I don't know. We kind of move around a lot."

"Oh." I wasn't sure what to say, the house I lived in now was the only one I'd ever known. "That's cool," I said, only the way I said it wasn't cool.

Cullen chuckled. "Yeah, I guess." He snapped up to his feet. Before I could get up he was tromping across the suspension bridge.

I started across the bridge, where he was already gauging a tall pine tree. It was maybe fifty or sixty feet tall, with sharp, broken limbs like pegs all the way up. I held onto the railing, continuing my careful advance across the bridge. Then, Cullen leaped up to the first broken branch, where he hurled himself up.

He held out his arms for balance. "So," he said, looking down to me. "You coming?"

I shook my head. I wasn't big on climbing trees or heights in general. Cullen scampered up to the next limb, then, like a ladder, hoisted himself up again and again. I hurried over to the base of the tree, craning my neck as I gazed straight up. My mind did what it did best. I worried about Cullen's peeling Vans. What if they caused him to trip? Same for the chain dangling on one side, snagging a branch. What about the headphone cord around his neck? There were too many head-spinning possibilities.

Cullen didn't seem to have these worries, not by the way he climbed to the top and settled between two limbs, feet dangling, looking as though he were sitting on a park bench.

"The view is pretty awesome up here," he called down.

"I'll take your word for it." My knees wobbled just looking up that far.

When we got back on our street, Cullen stopped in front of his house. The hood was up on the Buick, and I heard the winding of a ratchet. I craned my neck, only able to see the tattooed arm holding the ratchet. Cullen popped the cassette from his Walkman. "Here," he said, handing it to me.

"What's this?"

"The Beastie Boys. Trust me, you'll like it."

"Thanks," I said to Cullen, flipping over the cassette where he'd scrawled *Check Your Head* in marker over the fuzz of a peeled off sticker. I slid it in my pocket and nodded. Behind the hood of the car, Cullen's dad looked up but didn't wave. He was a big guy, bearing little resemblance to Cullen, bald with a scruffy beard and a big gut stretching out his oil-stained shirt.

Cullen turned back to him and headed for the door. "All right man, see ya."

And that was that.

———

DINNER WAS LEFTOVER PASTA. Mom was too worked up to handle anything else as the Democratic Convention was set to get underway. She flitted about the kitchen, whipping up a garlic spread as we took our places at the table. Dad griped about his day—his crew was finishing up a church restoration, and he mentioned something about the pews not being the right size. I waited for Mom to mention the Mega More, but she only nodded along.

Dad went for a piece of bread and took his first shot. "So what time does the delusional convention start?"

Mom didn't even blink. "At eight o'clock, our future president will speak."

"Oh please. I hardly think that the American people are going to put some hick from Arkansas in office," Dad said. I glanced her way.

"I think the people of this country are more than ready to get back on track."

"On track? How? By taxing and spending?" Dad was already flailing. His arms and hands took flight when he got worked up.

For the next thirty minutes my parents spoke in a language I could hardly follow. They spanned the constitution, Watergate, Desert Storm, before settling on Iran Contra, which led to my dad's hero, Mr. Ronald Reagan.

My dad loved Ronald Reagan like a grandfather. He was fond of saying that the only reason he voted for Bush was because he couldn't vote for Reagan a third time. Whenever he said it, Mom went on a head-shaking rant about poverty and working wages.

I drifted off, thinking about Cullen and how I was going to get him to show me some tricks on my skateboard.

After a shower I found my parents all settled in on the couch for the convention. Mom was serious about watching this thing; she'd taken the phone off the hook and plopped down on the couch with a bowl of homemade trail mix. I grabbed a handful and took my place on the floor, picking out the almonds and laughing because Dad had this goofy look stuck to his face. Mom slapped his knee whenever he opened his mouth to speak.

For all the build-up, things were kind of boring. At least when my parents watched *Larry King Live* callers chimed in to offer opinions, but this thing was just one big love fest. Everyone there had the same starry-eyed trance Mom wore on her face. The sections were broken down by states, and New York looked to be the rowdiest. They were going nuts. Finally, after nearly an hour of yapping and blathering, Mom cranked up the volume until the floor model rattled as Bill Clinton took to the large *DC '92* podium, waving and strutting like a rock star.

It took nearly ten minutes for him to nod and wave and thank everyone. And whenever it looked like he was finally going to get a chance to speak, they would crank up again with all the applause and chanting. Dad chuckled and snickered until Mom shot him a shotgun stare, and his end of the couch went quiet.

I didn't know much about Bill Clinton, but the guy was smooth. He had this way about him that was both gentle and stern as he talked about nation building and change. He told stories of his grandfather and his mother and life in his small town. Even Dad admitted that he was good, but he said so in a way that didn't sound much like a compliment.

Mom was zapped into silence. She hung on every word, her

hazel eyes fixed on the Zenith, nodding and whispering in agreement as the governor looked right into our living room and spoke about struggling families, working people, and the middle class. He spoke of the ten million out of work and the continuing rise of unemployment. Mom laughed so hard she snorted when he said that our president should be the next one out of work.

That woke her up. She pumped her fist and cheered him on when he spoke of women's rights and equality. Again, Dad started to say something but was shut down before he could get a word in.

When the news people started dissecting the speech, I escaped to my room, letting Mom and Dad debate Mr. Clinton's performance. I liked what he'd said, but from what Dad had told me, I liked George Bush too. Which brought me back to the same old question: How could they both be wrong? Or right?

10

I woke up in the middle of the night, legs burning, screaming with an urgent need to be scratched. The more I scratched the more it itched, until my sanity teetered, and I thought about chopping my legs off at the knees or maybe just the ankles. Anything would be better than this.

Flopping over, rain pelted the window as the sky flickered. A few seconds later came a deep rumble I felt in my bed. But nothing took my mind off the agony covering my skin, in the folds where my knees bent, all over my bony ankles. Chiggers, or Trombiculidae, as my mom sometimes called them with flourish. Basically, mites. It happened every summer.

I clawed at my legs, my mouth stretching open from the pleasure and pain. And once I got started there was no stopping. The itch only strengthened with each scrape of my nails. It was dark so I couldn't see, I may have been ripping the skin off my legs.

My mind roamed with ideas, instruments to scratch my legs. The bristles of a hairbrush, the teeth of my house key—a chainsaw might do the trick. One thing was for sure, getting back to sleep wasn't going to happen. Hopping up, I felt my way around my desk, finding my Swatch. It was 3:56 in the morning.

All I could do was scratch. The worst was around my ankles, but it ran up my legs, around my waist, other places, too. Turning on my lamp, my skin was ruddy, lined with scratch marks around the bumps with crimson dots.

Somehow I did manage to fall asleep. When I woke up again it was light outside. I was on my floor, the bedspread bunched up around my ankles. I pulled it away, my legs were covered with dots, some scabbed over from my assault.

After breakfast I twitched and flinched as I tried to ignore the itch. Mom had given me a piece of the Aloe plant she kept in the bathroom. I rubbed it onto my legs as I sat on the couch, watching an ESPN special on the Dream Team, when Cullen strolled in the house and fell onto the couch beside me.

"Your mom said I could come in, so…"

I nodded, biting down hard on my lip. Cullen looked down and then smiled. "She said you were in bad shape."

"Yeah. Argh. These things itch so bad." I scanned his khakis, where his legs held scabs and scrapes in various stages of repair. "They didn't get you?"

He shook his head. "Nope. I guess I'm too fast," he said, karate chopping the air.

The TV flashed to highlights of Jordan and Pippen, then Magic and Bird. Cullen looked to the screen, where it skipped to an interview with MJ.

"Who's that?" Cullen asked.

I laughed. "Um. That's Michael Jordan."

"Oh."

I waited for a punchline of some sort, because I'd never met anyone who didn't recognize, much less had never heard of Michael Jordan. But Cullen only sat staring blankly until I smacked my legs—trying a new technique, but that wasn't working well either.

Suddenly Cullen's face lit up and he turned to me, like he'd just remembered something. "Hey, I know something to fix that."

I shook my head. "What? Nail polish? Bleach mix? I've tried it all."

"No, something way better. It's an old homemade remedy. Something my grandmother used to make for us." He moved to the window to peek outside, where Mom tugged away at weeds. "Let's go to the kitchen, see if you have the right...ingredients."

At that point I was game for anything. I led Cullen to the kitchen, where he went right for the fridge. He put a finger to his chin as he took inventory of the all-natural condiments and sauces.

"Hmm," he said tapping his chin. "I think we can make this work."

"Really?" I'd already plopped down on the floor, scratching away. "I hope so."

Even being preoccupied with my legs I thought it was strange when he grabbed the baking soda. The next thing I knew he was back in there, scooping things out by the armload: Miracle Whip, Greek yogurt, soy milk, a stick of butter, a jar of pickles, a garlic clove, applesauce, and the pure maple syrup. He piled the contents on the counter and spun around. "Where's your peanut butter? You're not allergic, right?"

"What?" I glanced around. "No. Why?"

"Do you want to stop itching?" he asked. Before I could reply he spun around to the pantry. "Hmm, crunchy or creamy? I guess it doesn't matter. Grandma always used creamy."

I pointed to the cabinet, where he snatched the peanut butter, then, after some deliberation, went back to the fridge for the seedless blackberry jelly Mom had made last week.

"Okay, I think this will do it," he said, rubbing his hands together. "Now I need a mixing bowl."

I motioned to the cabinet, and before I had time to even think about what was going on, Cullen was sitting cross-legged on the floor, tongue out in concentration as he went to work. He dumped in the baking soda, adding water and stirring it in until it was like a paste. After that he splashed in a dab of pickle juice, four shakes of salt, three shakes of pepper, two heaping spoonfuls of Miracle Whip, followed by a half a stick of butter, and then—with a shrug—the other half.

"Are you sure this will work?" I asked, too hopeful to be skeptical. Like a surgeon, he held his hand out, asking for the syrup. He mixed and mashed, and the murky substance in the bowl turned into a thick, caramel-colored batter.

"Okay, you ready? Give me your leg," he said, reaching for my foot. He'd found Mom's yellow cleaning gloves under the sink and had them yanked clear to his elbows. Between the gloves and the smile creeping up his cheeks, he looked a little like a mad scientist. And yet still, like a lab rat, I did as I was told.

Before I had a chance to think about what was happening, he scooped a glop of the paste and smeared it down my calf. It was cold and gritty, but soothing on my skin.

This might work, I thought, as Cullen slathered the stuff on generously, all over the red dots, until it kind of felt like a cast. I took the moment to ask him about skating. "Oh, so uh, I was wondering if you could show me some of those skateboard tricks," I said as he worked.

He nodded, his face straining with concentration. "Yeah, sure man. Of course."

After smothering my right leg, he went to work on the left. His lips pulled tight as he slathered on a generous dose of his grandmother's spackle to my foot. The cast on my right leg was starting to harden, cracking as I wiggled my toes. When Cullen told me to hold still, his voice was off, his hands trembling.

"Hey, are you okay?" I asked. The way he sat, his head down, his shoulders shaking, I thought he might be crying. Maybe he was thinking about his grandmother. Maybe the old recipe had stirred up old memories from his childhood that were too painful to think about.

"Cullen?"

He waved his hands in front of his face, and I was about to ask if he was okay again when he fell over onto his side, smacking the floor and rolling over onto his back as tears of laughter streamed toward his ears.

I looked at my legs, then to the bowl of crud. I closed my eyes.

Man was I a sucker.

"Dude, I can't believe you let me do that," he said between laughing fits. He grabbed the peanut butter, shaking his head. "I kept waiting for you to stop me." More gasping. "Garlic? Pickle juice?"

Cullen was heaving and gasping when Mom swung into the kitchen. She stopped as she saw us on the floor. "What in the world?"

Her eyes swept over the trail of condiments, to the cloud of flour hanging in the air, and then finally to the two edible casts on my legs. A smirk parted her lips. "Okay. What's going on?"

Cullen sat up, wiping the tears from his face. "Sorry, we were trying a home remedy. A family recipe of mine." He could barely get the words out.

I rolled my eyes. Mom laughed, shaking her head. "Well, is it working?"

"Maybe. I'm not thinking about scratching."

She leaned down, pressed a finger to my leg, and then brought it to her lips to taste. "Hmm, needs a little sugar," she said and stepped over our mess toward the sink.

Mad as I was, it didn't last. Not when Cullen spent almost every day at our house. The funny thing was how he actually listened to Mom's rants about Mega More like he was interested. He even signed her petition. I withheld my signature, because it was kind of a conflict of interest.

Mom said she understood.

ON FRIDAY AFTERNOON, Danny's mom drove us out to the Cineplex to see Encino Man. On the ride over Danny was all worked up about the upcoming Little League baseball season. He said his dad wanted to get me out there playing this year, maybe put me in at left field and help me out with my swing. That sounded great and all, but Coach had said the same thing last year.

With everything going on, I hadn't even thought about baseball this year. And now, as Danny went on about sign-ups, all I could think was how watching from the sweltering dugout all over again this year sounded like a big old waste of time. Working in my favor was how Dad was too preoccupied with Mega More to even bring it up.

"Nice shorts," Danny said, nodding to the Duckheads I'd recently sheared from pants I'd outgrown. Mrs. P peeked back in the rear-view, asked if I got in a fight with the garden shears.

I laughed it off, but I couldn't help thinking how when I was hanging out with Danny, everything was about sports, which used to be great because sports were my life. But lately I'd found that there were other things to do, and it wasn't the end of the world if I never did get out on the field or play baseball at all. It was hard to explain, but suddenly everything had changed.

When I hung out with Cullen, I never knew what would happen. One day he was excited about a new album of some band that I'd never heard of, and the next day he was pulling that prank with my legs—I was still scrubbing the baking soda off my ankles.

After the movie, Danny and I strolled around the mall. He ogled over all the sneakers in the shoe store, while I found myself looking out the windows, bored even though the new Olympic Air Jordan's had arrived and were out on display with a bright red tag that read $120. Dream Team? More like dream on. After stopping for Lemonheads and other contraband, we found Mrs. Peebles at Sears and made our way to the van.

When we got back to my house, Dad was outside, elbow deep in a cloud of charcoal dust, cleaning the grill. Mrs. Peebles pulled in behind the Renault, Mom's blazing white Clinton/Gore sticker screaming for attention. Mrs. Peebles waved to Dad as she spoke to me. "So has your father managed to talk *any* sense into your mother yet?"

"Oh, uh, I don't think so," I said, hoping she hadn't seen the petition.

"Well, the Peebles are *excited* about the store," she said as though that should settle everything. Danny asked if I wanted to grab some stuff and sleepover, but the last thing I wanted to do was spend the rest of my evening defending Mom. And when I spotted Cullen out in the street, riding wheelies on his bike, I made up a story about all the chores I had to do.

Danny glanced down the street then shook his head. He said he'd see me at practice. Just as soon as the van backed out of the driveway, I grabbed my skateboard and ran down to meet up with Cullen, determined to learn how to do that kick-flip even if it killed me.

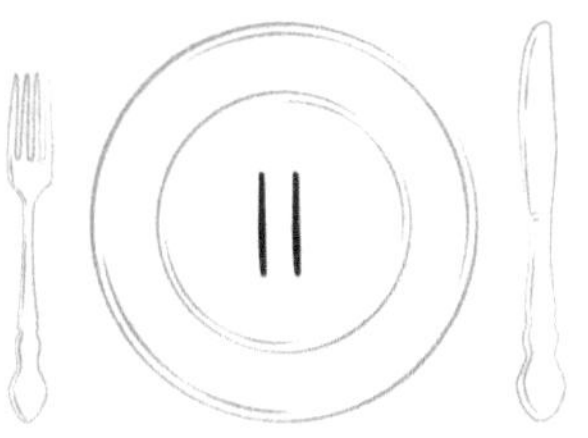

On Saturday morning I cracked my eyelids and found my dad looming in the doorway. "Marcus. Oh good, you're up. I thought you could come and give me a hand today."

I sat up on my elbow, rubbing my eyes. Two minutes after seven and here was Dad, chipper as ever in his usual pocket t-shirt, jeans, and work boots.

"At work?" I asked, still hoping this was some bad, but realistic dream. Dad smiled, nodded, then took a sip of realistic smelling coffee.

"Well, yeah, figured you could help me out. I need to check on a few things around town," he said, tapping the door with his wedding ring. "We're leaving in ten minutes." My head hit the pillow.

Twenty minutes later we pulled into Bramblewood Baptist Church. Dad parked beside a battered van with ladders on the roof. I hopped out of the truck, hearing some banging around inside the church. Two teenagers hauled a pew out the front doors that were propped open like butterfly wings.

"How's it coming along, guys?" Dad said in his foreman voice, which wasn't too different than the "Eat your peas" tone he used at the dinner table. The long-haired guy gave a bleary nod.

"We just got here."

Dad grimaced. He did that at dinner too. They dropped the pew beside the others.

"Okay, is Hank here?" Dad inquired. The guy shook his head. Dad took a deep breath and motioned for me to follow him inside.

Our steps echoed in the stripped and hollowed-out church. Where the pews had been yanked out, you could see their outline on the scarred wooden floors. The bullet-shaped stained-glass windows had been removed, and sawdust danced in the shafts of sunlight streaming through the empty arches.

I looked up to the exposed wires in the rafters. "Why are you ripping everything out of the old church?"

"Well," Dad said, following my gaze. "We're taking what can be salvaged before we tear it down."

The two teenagers started on the bolts fastened to the next set of pews. They were about halfway toward the door.

"They're tearing it down?" I asked, peering through one of the windows.

"Well, yeah," Dad said. "The church is expanding. We'll build a new one in its place. Only it will be about double the size."

We'd passed the old church a thousand times, usually without notice, but sometimes, in the evening, the stained-glass windows caught the sunlight with a glow. Now the chilly morning breeze swirled about the gutted sanctuary. "What about the windows?" I said, and dad turned to the empty slots.

"Went to a collector in Maryland."

"Oh," I said, looking around the church. "How old is this place?"

"Built in 1888. You should see some of the stuff we found in the basement." Dad lowered his head to get my attention. "Hey?" He studied my face then let out a sigh. "Marcus, I know your mom feels differently about some things. But, you see, this is progress."

"I know, but I've always liked this church."

I jumped as the two workers wrenched another pew from its place. They banged it free, lifted it out, and carried it through the propped-open doors, leaving a new front row. Dad put a hand on my shoulder. "Hey, remember when they built the new elementary school, and you got so excited because the lights were brighter and the blacktop was new, without the holes you had to avoid during kickball games? I mean, things change, Marcus. If they didn't, we'd still be in the dark ages—which sometimes I think would make your mom happy."

I nodded. "I know."

As we were leaving, Dad barked some orders to the rest of the guys. I waited in the truck, watching him as he watched them. All I could think about was what Mom would say about the old church at the creek. But Dad had a point, we couldn't keep *everything* forever. We had to move on.

Dad hopped in the cab and turned the key. When he did, I saw the purple scar under the bulge of his forearm—the only scar from his brush with death.

When I was five my dad was hit by a train. I'd made him tell me the story so many times over the years it felt like I was there. He was in his truck, crossing the railroad tracks on his way to work one morning, when his tires lost traction on the gravel. He was spinning out when, sure enough, a freight train came barreling down on him. Another mash of the gas, but the tires only dug deeper in the gravel. The conductor blasted his horn and pulled the brake, but there was no time. With nowhere to go, Dad dove to the passenger floorboard, scraping his arm on the gear lever just before the train sent the truck flying end over end until it came to rest on the embankment.

Mom still couldn't talk about the train without tearing up, and whenever someone heard about it they'd shake their heads, say how lucky he was to survive, to be t-boned by a locomotive and walk away with only a single gash on the arm. But not me. I thought he was Superman.

We took a couple detours on the way home. First, we swung by McDonald's for secret biscuits, then, as we got down the road, Dad took the turn toward Old Squabble Creek. I shot him a look, but he only grinned. "What? I need to show you a few things. It's better to have both sides of the story before you go sign that petition."

"You know about the petition?"

Dad laughed. "Of course I do."

"And you're not mad?"

He sighed. "Marcus, if I got mad at your mother for every time she stood up for her beliefs, we never would have made it to the altar."

We drove past the cemetery and entered through a newly blazed dirt road. My gaze followed the two-track gravel drive that Mom and I had biked down to the giant chestnut tree at the entrance. The warm McDonald's bag sat between us, and I wondered what Mom would think if she knew Dad was poisoning me—both mind and body.

I have to stop doing that, I told myself—thinking about one parent when I was spending time with the other one.

Dad cleared his throat. "Now, there's your cemetery," he said, pointing out the obvious. Then he swung his arm over the tall grass and wildflowers. "Now see all of those trees? They're staying put," he said, as though holding them up with his hands. "Keep looking now."

We drove for a few more seconds before slowing. "Okay. And here..." he said as we pulled over onto the newly flattened grass. "Here's where the dreaded Mega More will go. The construction of which will put many a fine vegetarian dinner on your plate."

The truck squeaked as we drove over toward the mill, where

a few felled trees lay by the weeds and brush. He set the truck in park and hopped out. I grabbed a biscuit from the bag and climbed out the other side, stuffing some extra napkins in my pocket. I scoped out a tree over by a rock pile—just in case.

"Now, where we're standing will be the parking lot," he said, lowering the tailgate. "And way over by that sagging fence, that's where the Mega More will start."

I took a seat, spanning the field, my gaze pausing at the cemetery. Only the top of that grand chestnut was visible over the tall weeds glistening in the warming sun. I wondered if he realized how peaceful it was right then, the birds chirping, the wind in the leaves. It was like we were having a nice picnic, until I heard Mom's voice in my head. *On the parking lot.*

I shook it off and focused on my dad. "Are you guys really going to move the creek? What about the influx of traffic?"

Dad smirked. "*Influx* of traffic?" He chuckled. "Did she give you a worksheet with this stuff?"

"It's on the petition," I said, clawing at my ankles.

Dad nodded. "Ah, okay. Well, the road will be widened. Lower Wilson will have trees, buffers, bike paths. I can show you the plans. We're not going to *move* the creek but redirect it. There will be a natural preserve, with walking trails—all part of the deal. Plus a stop light right back that way near Route 43. Now, did you need some maple syrup for your chiggers? I got a couple packets at McDonalds."

"Mom told you about that?"

"Classic," he said, wiping his face.

I tore into my biscuit. Something rustled near the river, and Dad and I both leaned closer. I thought maybe it was a deer or maybe even a stray dog, when suddenly a large, *something*, burst from the tree. It flew toward us with three or four great swooping flaps, a blur of blue and gray as it plunged down to the felled tree near our truck.

I stopped chewing, staring at the curled neck and cocked head, in awe of the massive, prehistoric bird. Its legs seemed fragile as straw, but the way it held its head, atop its long S shaped neck, its long beak and determined eyes, was anything but. I turned to Dad, who started to whisper, but the creature didn't stick around, flying off and flapping toward the cemetery. I couldn't be sure, but I thought I recognized the *Don't tell your mother* look that spread across my father's face.

We didn't stay long after that.

When we got home, Mom was on the carport, her nose buried in a book. "So, how did it go?"

"Good." I nodded, avoiding eye contact because I wasn't sure if our little trip to the build-site was a secret.

Dad fell into the seat beside her and came right out with it. "We went to the old church, then to a few other sites," he said, fiddling with the pages of a magazine. "Went by Squabble Creek, too."

Mom lowered her brick-thick book. "Oh? And how was that?"

I shrugged, thinking about the bird. Its yellowish beak, its talons, the huge wingspan. "Um, good, it's pretty far away from the cemetery."

The book shut with a thump. Feeling ambushed, I ducked out of the carport, where I spotted Cullen at the end of the driveway on his bike. He nodded his head from the street, and I snuck off as Mom and Dad got cranking. She was already on edge, with her big meeting with the city council on Tuesday—a last ditch effort to halt the construction. She'd somehow been able to wrangle her way up to nearly two-hundred signatures. Dad had laughed and told her to go right ahead, there was no way they would lose all that tax money.

Cullen pulled off his headphones, and I could hear the tinny sound of a guitar solo. "What's up man?" he said, looking over my shoulder to the carport. "So what are your parents talking about?"

"Oh, just...you know, Mega More."

Cullen smiled. "How we're going to stop them?"

"What?"

"Yeah. So hey, I've been meaning to ask you, let's go out there. I want to see the site."

"You do?" I kept thinking about the bird. Did it have a family, or flock, or whatever the heck it was called? I didn't even know what sort of bird it was.

He shrugged. "Why not?"

I grabbed my bike. Mom was on the edge of her seat, railing about endangered species. Dad scoffed, and the situation looked to be heating up. When I caught up with Cullen he gave me that devious grin. "Oh, so check it out, I got us a job."

I thought about my morning with Dad. "*Us?*"

"Yeah, your babysitter," he said, motioning down to Caitlyn's house. "Her parents hired me to cut their grass."

"She's not my babysitter." At least not anymore. But what I was really thinking was, how in the world did he pull that off?

12

On the eve of Mom's big city council meeting, Mr. Reynolds, of Reynolds Construction Company, thought it would be good practice to have a spokesman present at the meeting to counter Mom's argument and speak in favor of the project. From what Dad mentioned, Mr. Reynolds wanted to get the company's side of things on the record, or as Mom later put it, to remind the council members of the big financial windfall coming their way.

It just so happened they chose my dad as that spokesman.

Did the construction company understand the industrial-sized burden they were placing on my dad's square shoulders? Did they think it was mere coincidence the two of them had the same last name? I can't say, but it made life in our house all the more awkward when he came home with the news last night.

Dad figured the meeting would all be over in twenty-minutes tops. He said there was no way Council would change their mind. A Mega More Super Store was coming to town. It was a done deal.

That afternoon I peeked in on Mom at her desk. She looked up and smiled. "Hey sweetie, how are your chores coming along?"

I shrugged. "Oh, you know, having a blast."

Mom gave me a warm smile and removed her glasses. I leaned over her shoulder and asked, "How's it coming along?"

"Good," she said. "It's just, this whole thing with your dad being there. It might get a little weird."

I raised my eyebrows. That was an understatement. "Do you think they'll change their mind?"

She sighed. "Probably not, but at least I'm doing something. I couldn't live with myself if I didn't try. I'd spend the rest of my life regretting it."

Weird didn't describe what happened next. Mom was setting the table for an early dinner when Dad stormed in the front door. He hustled over and kissed her on the cheek. "Is this the last supper?"

Mom fluttered her eyes like a good little homemaker and not someone trying to ruin his biggest project at work. "Anything for my loving husband, dear."

He jerked his face away from hers, his arms falling to her waist. "You do know I love you, right?" Mom nodded with a smile. They were still locked in a loving embrace when he kissed her cheek again. "But tonight, I will have to squash your little plans, dear."

"We'll see."

After a quick shower Dad returned to the kitchen, fixing the cuffs of his button-down shirt. Mom whistled as she reached over and fixed his tie. "Well, you sure clean up nicely."

Dad rolled his eyes, then widened them when he noticed Mom had changed into a navy-blue blouse and skirt. "Well Mrs. Hawthorne, you look incredible."

Then they kissed. Like I said, weird, strange, bizarre. Gross. I took my seat at the table with these two characters. Mom set out the mandarin chicken and rice. It was all kind of ridiculous, a sit-down family dinner before war. I scooped out a tiny bit of the chicken, because once again Mom had been too preoccupied to cook anything decent.

"Are we riding together?" I asked.

Dad's smile went south. "Well, I hadn't planned on it. That might get kind of dicey, don't you think, Ana?"

Mom flicked her hair back. "I thought it might be nice. We could go for ice cream afterwards?"

"The fellas are going to love this one," Dad mumbled.

"What's that, dear?"

Dad dropped the act, setting his fork on the table. "Do you know how much flak I'm catching at work? How am I supposed to earn respect when my own wife is pulling a stunt like this?"

We interrupt our regularly scheduled programming to report a skirmish erupting at the Hawthornia border. At any moment this thing could break wide open...stay tuned...

Mom cocked her head. "A stunt? That's what you think this is? *A stunt?* I'm standing up for what I believe in."

"And you're going to run me out of work by doing so," Dad said, a bit too loud before he caught himself. He held up his hands and lowered his voice. "Ana, this is my job."

With great effort, I stabbed a bite of chicken and took my first bite, watching as Mom glowered at Dad. "Fine. I won't go."

She scooted her chair back slowly, wiped her mouth, and tossed her napkin to the table. Dad watched her with regret in his eyes. I'd never seen my mom give up, but when she walked out of the room, down the hall where she shut the door, everything fell silent.

Dad plowed in with a bite of chicken, grimaced and then smiled at me with a half-hearted attempt at conversation. "So, the lawn looks good."

"Dad."

"And your room, is it clean?"

"*Dad.*"

He took a super deep breath and nodded. "I know, I know."

His napkin hit his plate like a white flag. He stood, took a breath, then limped down the hall. I crept to the doorway of the kitchen, only able to hear muffled voices behind the bedroom door. An exchange, then softer, and then finally faint and fleeting. But about three minutes later, the door swung open and Mom marched down the hallway.

"Get dressed, Marcus, we're leaving."

W e slid into Dad's truck, continuing the strangest evening of my life. Mom scooted past the plans and papers to the middle seat, wiping at her skirt. I could tell she was worried about all the red dirt and dust but wasn't about to say a word about it.

As for me, I'd managed to pass under her radar in a semi-wrinkled collared shirt and a pair of jeans that had been hanging in my closet since school let out. Between the flare up at dinner and this city council meeting, I think I could have gotten away with wearing a bathrobe and she wouldn't have noticed. With both my parents addressing the council, I was instructed to sit in the back and not to make a peep, which was fine by me because I was still trying to stay neutral in this whole thing.

At a stoplight, Dad took a break from his steering wheel tapping to crane his neck toward the mirror and adjust his necktie. Mom looked him over.

"I love that shirt on you, Ben. It brings out your eyes."

Dad smiled, leaning over and kissing her on the cheek. I groaned.

"Green light, Dad."

We started down the road and I shook my head, playing with the tape measure and making a silent vow never to get married.

After parking downtown, I walked behind my two well-dressed parents, who swung their locked hands in step, ready for battle—with each other. Dad had his rolled-up plans under his arm, and Mom had her manila folder with all her notes and legal pad scrawlings.

Entering the lobby, an old man with gray stubble on his face stood and nodded to my mom. Dad grinned at her.

"Part of your legal team?"

"This is where we part, hon. Good luck," she said with a smile. Then she turned to me. "Marcus, go through the double doors and find a seat in the back, okay, sweetie?"

In the back, I thought, as though I might be hit with shrapnel or mortar shells. I nodded, watching as she and the old-timer fell into a whispered discussion. Though he was old, the man looked fit and spry, like he was ready to climb a mountain. And his eyes were intense, burning like two searchlights.

Dad put a hand on my back. "I hope you know that this is all business. And remember, this is my job."

"Good luck," I said, heading for the chambers. The heavy doors echoed loudly as they closed. The plush carpet was like a cushion under my sneakers as I slid into a spot along the empty row in the back.

Chambers described it perfectly. The floor sloped down to a gigantic, curved desk with five wing-backed chairs, like a throwaway set from Star Trek. Each place at the desk had its own little microphone in the spotlight. Centered on the back wall was the gold seal of East Ridge, with the plow in the field and the mountains in the distance. To the left, a state flag, to the right, the American flag.

Every movement and cough was amplified in the quiet murmur of the room. I scanned the few heads in the rows. A bald guy with neck rolls, an elderly lady, a couple of men in suits in the front row, some college-aged kids. And as the door opened and stayed open, more and more people found their way down the aisles.

While I sat waiting for something to happen—for my parents to enter and state their cases for and against the building of a brand new Mega More Super Store—I thought how summer was already a month gone. I still couldn't nail that kick flip on a skateboard, and now here I was wasting my time at a city council meeting.

Mom and the old guy walked in. She put a hand on the bench and gave me a bright smile that lit up the cavernous chamber. I nodded. More faithful citizens were trickling in, and by the time I saw Dad enter with a guy in a dark suit at his side, the place was half full.

Mom and Dad took their respective places. Mom with the old man on her side of the aisle, Dad, looking a bit pallid with the rest of the suits on the other. Up front, a side door swung open, and I got my first glimpse at the very *un*distinguished members of Newburg's City Council.

The five geezers took to their big spaceship chairs. Not sure what they'd been doing all this time back there, probably dosing off seeing how some of the comb-overs were hanging. Once they were settled in, the guy in the middle slipped some glasses on and shuffled his papers. When he spoke, I knew I was in for a long ride.

His nasally voice clawed my ears as he welcomed us to the special hearing. He droned on about taxing and planning, zoning and commercial use, and other sleep-inducing topics. I counted the tiles in the ceiling and was over a hundred before someone else finally got a turn to speak.

A small, confused looking man stood before the council and took the microphone—something about a license of some sort. The councilmen voted and the panel lit up like a video game. This happened several times until I was bored to exhaustion. I'd re-laced my left shoe and was starting on the right when at last, the leader guy announced it was time to address the matter regarding the Mega More site. By now, half the bleacher section was full—Dad's half.

This was it. I leaned forward, resting my forearms on the back of the bench in front of me, wishing I was closer. The middle guy asked if anyone wanted to speak in favor, although he made sure to squeeze in how the council had already voted in favor of the build back in November.

The procession began, as men and women scooted out of the pews, adjusted the microphone and basically repeated the same thing over and over again: Mega More was great for the community. Jobs, taxes, resources, economical, and so on. It was like everyone was reading from the same script.

Then Dad stood. He fixed his collar and carefully made his way to the podium. But the guy in the fancy shirt was only a shell of the guy I knew. His movements were stiff and rigid. He cleared his throat and greeted the council members, his voice shaking as he fumbled through his notes and plans.

"Gentlemen...uh...um...I'm...Ben...Hawthorne...with... Reynolds...Bros. Construction...site has been zoned for commercial use."

I winced as my big, strong father stammered and sputtered. At least I was far enough away that I couldn't hear most of it because his voice was so low. But still, it was hard to watch. He moved like Frankenstein up there, a big oaf lumbering through his points, certainly nothing like the fun guy who tossed the ball around in the front yard. Near the end, with the councilmen's encouragement, he sort of found his groove, or at least he was able to string some sentences together. He wiped his forehead and looked down to his notes.

"Our estimates show that it would bring..."

He spouted off figures and the councilmen nodded with his

estimates. By the time he wrapped up, they were all smiles as they thanked him for his time. Dad wiped his forehead, grimaced, and lumbered back to his seat.

With no other speakers, the middle councilmember—who by then I'd gathered was our mayor—adjusted his glasses, turned to his notes, and with a hint of agitation in his voice, called my mom. "Ana Hawthorne."

I chuckled as he did a double take at the last name, checking the notes once again, his tiny chin lost somewhere in his wobbly cheeks. The bride of Frankenstein stood with a broad smile and strode to the podium. "Good evening, Councilmen," she said, her voice clear and crisp, stealing the attention of the room with its confidence. "Thank you for the opportunity to speak with you tonight."

She lowered the mic, her posture straight and her voice impeccable. She tossed back her hair and cocked her head to the side. My mom stood before the council, outnumbered, undermanned, and thoroughly unafraid. I swallowed hard, took a breath, and craned my neck for a better view because I knew, win or lose, things were about to get interesting.

"Preserving our history and the land which holds such history is a civic duty. We owe it not only to ourselves but to future generations to be the caretakers of the earth. Land was once a part of our lives, not something bought and sold to the highest bidder. One only needs to look to Appalachia—how the mountains were stripped and mined, left ragged and in ashes, useless to people who lived there—to see what can happen. Why the same people who worked those mines were left flooded and homeless."

The mayor leaned into the microphone. "Mrs. Hawthorne, while we appreciate your—"

"Mayor Pickens, I believe I have the floor," Mom said, her voice calm but sharp. My dad slid down in his chair. I couldn't stop the big fat grin that spread across my face as the mayor checked the clock with a nod.

"Uh, yes. Very well, then."

Mom let them hang there for a moment before she got back to business. "Tonight I'm here to plead with you, the council members, to halt the construction of the Mega More Super Store until a more suitable site can be found." She waved a hand to the seats. "While we've heard of all the wonderful benefits of having a monster chain store like Mega More in our community, those magnificent, low wage, non-unionized jobs it will bring to our town, I don't feel we've taken the time to study the disastrous effects..."

The mayor leaned forward to speak again but stopped short. Mom paused to let him squirm. I didn't need to see her face to know she was staring him down, her steely hazel eyes swimming with mischief. I'd seen it too many times at dinner. With her silent message sent, she resumed.

"We don't know the environmental effects on the wildlife, on the river that has flowed through our town since before we arrived. What about the impact of traffic and pollution, the desecration of graves? Councilmen, I implore you to consider this impact, to find a more suitable location for this eighty thousand square foot monstrosity."

All members of the council eyed the clock, now under ten seconds. They seemed to be urging it along. Mom saw it too.

"Now, let me end by saying that I do think there is a way for us to coexist, to embrace our natural history and move forward in our quest to bring businesses and tax revenue to our small community. Let's do this the right way. Thank you for your time, Councilmen."

Mom swept up her notes and turned for the aisle. She offered Dad a shining smile as she marched back to her bench.

The old man nodded and whispered into her ear. Mayor Pickens clumsily gripped his microphone.

"Uh, yes. Thank you, Mrs. Hawthorne. Now, if there aren't any other speakers, then I think we should vote. All in favor?"

All five hands rose. Mom's shoulders dropped.

"Okay, this meeting is adjourned."

I was in the living room, slogging through *Of Mice and Men,* when Dad's truck grumbled to a stop in the driveway. It was a little after five, and since I hadn't been able to find Cullen earlier, I'd wasted most of the afternoon plowing through my summer reading assignment. I set the book down as Dad, smiling like a kid, leaped out of the truck and started digging around in the truck bed. Then I saw why.

A sudden gasp sounded behind my back as Mom joined me. We watched as Dad produced a glossy *Bush/Quale '92* lawn sign and planted it in the yard like he'd just landed on the moon. After hammering down the stakes, he took a few steps back to make sure it was level. Then he turned to us, spreading his arms out wide with a smile.

Mom grunted. She cleared her throat as her voice struggled to find its proper pitch. "Well look at that," she said, her jaw set to a smile. Up until then Mom had taken the city council loss in stride, getting back to her editorials and writing. And up until then it seemed like Dad had known better than to rub it in her face.

Now, as he gave us a cheery wave, Mom waved back, slowly, still straining to smile. But through her teeth she mumbled some unsmiling things.

Negotiations could be tricky tonight, as a cat-and-mouse game has been underway since the warring factions of Hawthornia...developing...

At dinner, Dad's smile dropped as he regarded the colorful spread. Bruschetta topped with fat red tomatoes from the garden and basil she'd had me snip from the pot in the carport. The side dish was a Caesar Salad—no chicken this time—with large, crispy leaves spilling out of a wooden bowl. It was no secret in our house that my dad did not consider a meal to be complete without meat. And with that sign in the yard it was clear we were going to be vegetarians for the foreseeable future.

Or at least until this stupid election was over.

"Well, looks like we're eating light tonight," Dad said, picking out the largest piece of bread.

Mom forked out her salad with a smile. "I thought it was time for a nice, summery meal."

Her tone dripped with a sugary politeness that could only mean trouble. Dad snorted. I laughed too, cutting it short when Mom cut a meat-cleaver glare my way. I wiped my face and waited for whatever was coming. And it wasn't long before she cleared her throat and said, "Oh, so good news. I sold a piece to *Newsweek*."

Dad coughed. "*Newsweek*. Really?"

"Yep, five hundred big ones."

"Wow, Ana that's great," he said with a smile. He seemed genuinely impressed. At least until he gave it more thought. After another bite and chewing it over, his surprise turned to suspicion.

"So uh, what's the piece about?" he finally asked.

"The loss of mom and pop stores," Mom said between chews. "The homogenizing of America."

"Like what kind of milk they sell?" I asked.

Mom laughed. "Well, Marcus, you see, each town and region, rather, used to have its own unique feel, way of life, even speech. You could drive to different counties and hear different dialects, customs, and traditions. But now, with everything turning into one big strip mall, it's becoming all the same. We're losing our uniqueness."

Dad scoffed. "Ana, come on. Stop indoctrinating our kid."

"Oh yeah? Tell that to Dr. Zimmerman, whose research over a ten-year period clearly shows the correlation of large retail chains to the closing of smaller, family owned—"

Dad's hand smacked the table. "Oh please, save the psychobabble for your college professors and intellectuals. You know, it makes me wonder, has this Dr. Zimmerman ever set foot in one of these towns he studies? Has he ever worked a day in his life?"

"He's actually worked at the university for nearly twenty years. He's married and has three children, all of them grown, but..."

Dad wiped his mouth. "Not my point, Ana."

"Okay, so your point is...?"

Usually this was where I tuned out, when they started using big words and talking about studies. But lately I could tell Mom had been getting under Dad's skin. Like the public speaking thing, she was much more polished in her arguments. Dad, while full of good points and ideas, usually became too flustered to spit them out. He'd mutter and mumble before raising his voice when he got worked up. And when he started waving his hands, I knew he was all worked up.

"What I mean is, these *intellectuals* are the same people who protested Vietnam, who have spent a lifetime in the classroom and on campuses, while Joe Blue-collar busts his rump to get by."

"So you're saying that going to college—that education is a bad thing?"

Dad shook his head forcefully. "No, don't put words in my mouth. I mean, well, school is perfectly fine for some, but it's not for everyone."

"So I don't have to go to school?" I chimed in, spilling tomato slime on my shirt.

Mom slashed her eyes at me, then to my shirt. "Yes, of course you have to go to school."

Dad leaned back in his chair with a grin, setting his napkin by his plate. "Well, if he learns a trade, or wants to go into the military..."

Mom's jaw dropped. Dad looked pleased that he'd gained some ground. She pounced. "The military? Ben, have you lost your mind?"

"No, I would be proud if he served. My dad served. It's honorable, even if your hippie friends don't think so."

"My *hippie* friends?" Mom scoffed. "Ben, I protested Vietnam because we had no business being there. We lost so many lives, and for what?"

Dad leaned forward. "Look, Ana, all I'm saying is that..." He reached his hand out and set it on my mom's, his voice softening. "We did the city council thing, and I was supportive, but it's over now. Can't we move on?"

"So you're telling me what I can and can't write? You want me to stand to the side and be a good little homemaker while you destroy the very things I'm trying to preserve? I can't do that, Ben. You knew that when you married me."

A powerful silence fell over the room. Mom's eyes glistened under the chandelier. Dad's face held a rigidness I hadn't seen before. Ever since the city council meeting, it felt like a dark cloud had hung over the house. Now the storm raged.

"I think I'm finished," I said, and they both turned to me like they'd forgotten I was in the room. Things got quiet as I picked up my plate and carried it to the sink. They were still staring at each other when I left the kitchen.

In my room, I hopped on my bed, grabbing my Walkman and strapping on my headphones. Then I let the sounds of the Beastie Boys drown out the silence.

There was this eerie little song on the tape called "Something's Gotta Give." It had all these weird effects and noises in the background and it almost sounded like they were singing underwater. I listened to it twice, because it was exactly how I felt after the big fight at dinner.

While I waited for the tape to rewind, there was a knock at my door. Mom peeked in and Dad hovered over her in the doorway. "Hey sweetie, you okay?"

I pulled the headphones to my neck. "Yeah."

"Okay, we were just worried, you know, how we got a little carried away in there," Mom continued, talking to me like a baby.

Dad gave me a lopsided grin, his hands above his head on the doorframe. "Yeah, it was only a discussion."

I nodded. "Sounded more like a fight." I wasn't about to let them off the hook. Just because they argued every night didn't make me feel any better.

"No, it wasn't a fight. We just got going," Dad said, massaging Mom's shoulders.

"Do you want to watch TV or hang out?" Mom asked.

I nodded at the clock. "Let me guess, Crossfire? No thanks."

Mom smiled. She walked over to me and kissed the top of my head. Then she returned to Dad, hugging his waist.

"Hey," I called, and they both turned to me. "Do you guys agree on anything?"

Dad laughed. Mom looked at Dad then back to me with a smile. "Well, we both love you very much."

Dad hit the brakes hard as we backed out of the driveway, nearly clipping the monumental *Clinton/Gore '92* billboard at the edge of our lawn. A few days ago Mom had countered his sign with her own, staking it down in the yard while he was at work.

"That thing is a hazard," Dad grumbled as we started up the street. Mom winked at me and smiled. It never ended with them.

Politics aside, today was all about having fun. Every Fourth of July since I could remember, we'd gone to the Independence Day roast over at Peak's Park. Pretty much the whole town gathered for the event, and that was what had me more than a little worried as we started up the road.

We arrived around three on what must have been the hottest day of summer yet. As we parked, the crowd cheered on the baseball game from the lawn chairs clumped together under the shade, as older folks sipped lemonade and watched the Pepsi vs. Coke little league battle from a distance. And I could've been mistaken, but my mom was looking like a relief pitcher the way she loosened up her own arm as we stepped out of the car.

The park was decked out with patriotic flags and ribbons. Huge, drooping red, white, and blue buntings adorned the concession stands and food trucks, and Olympic *Team USA* signs were posted on the trees and fences. There were pony rides and kiddie games and a delicious smell in the air as the smoke plumed from the grills as all the BBQ and burgers and hot dogs a town could eat sizzled to perfection. But the Peak's Park Independence Day Roast was best known for a tradition that went back as far as when my dad was a kid: The Dunk-the-Mayor booth.

The baseball tournament was already underway. Even from the parking lot I could tell it was Danny on the pitcher's mound by the way he kicked at the dirt and adjusted his hat. Then he'd kind of stretch his neck and arch his back. For the past two summers I'd donned the Pepsi Pirates uniform to take my spot on the bench, so I knew the next pitch would be his curve.

Dad made a few comments about how it was weird not to see me out there this year, but Mom wasn't about to let him force me to play sports. He struck off to greet a few guys from work with insults and grunts. I hung back with Mom. Danny whipped a curve ball that smacked the catcher's mitt for a strike. It was then I noticed most of the faces in the chairs were tuned in on us. "Mom, why is everyone staring at you?"

Mom rolled her shoulders. "Oh, no reason," she said, her eyes spanning the grounds, locking in on the mayor who was sitting with his constituents in the bleachers, trying to cheer for both pitcher and batter. Mom mumbled to herself and then whipped around. "Where is that ticket booth?"

"Did you write another editorial?" I asked, just as the catcher's mitt clapped once again. This time Danny's pitch was called outside. "You did, didn't you?"

"Maybe," she said and then grabbed my arm. "Oh, there it is, come on."

We threaded through the crowd toward the concessions trailer. "Was it about the meeting?"

"People have a right to know the truth, Marcus," she said, jerking me along like I was a wagon full of water and she was headed for a fire.

"But why do we need tickets? You know I don't have an arm," I said, looking back at old Mayor Pickens, dabbing his forehead, yukking it up with the townsfolk. Mom stepped forward to the small window. That's when I heard a familiar voice.

"Yo, Marcus." I turned around to find Cullen, straddling his rusty bike, an oversized *Alice in Chains* t-shirt hanging loosely to his usual cut offs.

"Hey Cullen."

"So, this is all very small town," he said, looking around. But all I saw was my dad, knifing toward us, his face redder than sunburn. Mom stuffed a string of tickets long enough to circle the Earth into her purse. Cullen set his bike against a tree and we scooted up closer to see what was going on.

Dad leaned toward Mom. "Ana, could I have a word with you?"

"Oh. Sure, honey," she said, collecting her change from the smirking teenager who promptly flipped a *Sold-Out* sign on the window. As my parents scurried off to the parking lot, I looked to Mayor Pickens, still whooping it up with the old-timers. Cullen nudged me.

"Dude, your mom let the mayor have it in the paper."

"What?" I said. "I thought you didn't follow the news." I looked around, wondering how in the world I hadn't thought to check out the newspaper.

"Well, I do now." He leaned closer. "She accused him of being a sell-out. Man, how rad is your mom?"

I'd never spent much time pondering my mom's radness, but my stomach flipped and folded as the faces in the bleachers turned their attention to the parking lot, where my parents were engaged in a heated discussion behind the truck.

"This is not good," I said, glancing around.

"Aw snap!" Cullen shook me as our jubilant mayor hobbled

down the bleachers and grabbed a big beach towel, making a jolly show of his march to the Dunk-the-Mayor booth. "Dude, I think..."

"What?"

Cullen glanced at the *Sold Out* sign, then back to the parking lot. When he turned to me with a grin, there was nothing but trouble in his eyes. "I think your mom is going to drown the mayor."

Sure enough, Mom and Dad made their way back to the festivities. Mom with a pleasant smile and Dad looking like he'd gone a few rounds with Mike Tyson. The baseball game was called to an end, Pepsi upending their rivals 8-3. The two teams lined up in the infield for the "good game" hand smack, and I realized how little I missed it. Meanwhile, the crowd headed toward the picnic area and the stage, where the world's oldest bluegrass band was nodding off to sleep.

I tried not to think about whatever my mother was plotting and instead followed Cullen over to the nitrate stand. We ordered two dogs each, with the spicy hot chili, sure to do in my already problematic stomach. Sure enough, as soon as that first mouthful hit my gut it was kind of like how it felt as my two worlds collided when we ran smack dab into Danny, still sweaty and in uniform, eyeing Cullen.

"So Marcus, what's up with your mom? She's not going to give it a rest?"

My gaze fell to my chili dogs, sitting sloppy and warm on the thin paper plate. Coach Peebles wasn't far away, chatting with parents. For some reason I'd never realized how ridiculous he looked in his Pepsi Sluggers uniform before that day. Danny's gaze bounced from me to Cullen then back. All I could do was shrug. "I don't know, man, she's just—" *Getting ready to drown the mayor*, I almost said.

"She needs to realize that most people like stores," Danny

continued, which was weird because since when did he care so much?

"People like history, too," Cullen said between bites of his chili dog. And I'm not sure how he did it, but he even made that sound cool. Danny regarded Cullen like he was a space traveler. Then he turned back to me.

"Look, nobody cares about some podunk road or tiny cemetery that most people don't even know exists."

"We know. And the families of the deceased know," Cullen said defiantly, before finishing his first hot dog and wiping his mouth.

The deceased? Wow. I took a breath. Danny's brow furrowed, and his cheeks flushed the way they did when he was on the pitcher's mound and behind on the count. I motioned to Cullen. "Uh, this is Cullen. Cullen, this is Danny."

Danny nodded absently. When he spoke again his voice was friendlier, even if what he said was not. "Okay dude, I gotta go. But I might as well tell you, nobody really wants your mom here." He spun around and marched off, finding his dad and his teammates. Coach Peebles looked right at me and didn't even wave or nod. Like I was some stranger.

"Pfft, don't listen to that dude, he's just like the rest of them."

I didn't know what to say. *The rest of them?* I *was* them. I'd gone to kindergarten and slept over at their houses. I'd known them most of my life. But the way Cullen said *them*, it made me think sides had been drawn—like at my house. Like the election. It seemed everybody knew where they stood but me.

But there was no time to dwell on it because Mayor Pickens —who didn't need much help looking like a doofus—took to the loudspeaker and started grandstanding, even as he wore oversized goggles and scuba gear. He announced to the crowd that he was taking his place in the dunk booth.

"I challenge all of you slack-armed citizens to step up and give me your best shot!"

After being helped into the dunk seat—his wobbly cheeks sloshing around with the water in the tank—he positioned himself and called out to Carolyn Peters. "Now Carolyn, you might as well set those three baseballs down and let someone with an arm have a shot."

Carolyn chuckled, as did the rest of the well-intentioned citizens of our town who'd bought tickets to dunk the mayor. At three throws for a dollar, all proceeds went to the local chapter of the Humane Society. Someone in the crowd said it had been a record-breaking haul this year.

I forgot about my second hot dog as I edged closer to the action. I knew I had to find Mom, as one after another, the old-timers stepped up and lobbed baseballs that fell short of the booth. Taking turns, laughing and making light-hearted jokes about the mayor—who Mom said had run unopposed for the past three elections—they hurled soft lobs that didn't even come close to the target.

"I sure wish someone could throw a strike, I'm getting awfully hot up here," the mayor joked as floating baseballs missed far and wide, most coming up well short. Then, as the laughter gave way to an excited murmur and the crowd clamored about before parting for the next contestant, I found my mother, all five feet of her, marching right up to the throw line and fishing a handful of red tickets from her purse.

Oh boy. Cullen howled with laughter as we fought through to the ropes. The crowd tightened around us as she handed the volunteer a pile of tickets and readied herself without ever taking her eyes off of her target. The mayor's goofy grin collapsed like a cheap tent in a storm. Mom took a worn baseball in her hand as she and Mr. Pickens locked eyes like two duelers at dusk. The volunteer backed away, scrambling for cover.

Skipping the pleasantries, Mom cocked back like Roger Clemons and came down with a slider.

Whack.

She missed by a mile, thunking a maple tree thirty feet to the left and nearly beaning Glenda Ferguson, one of the Jaycees who sat gorging on a funnel cake. Glenda screamed through a mouthful of bread as the ball fell to her feet like a bruised apple, rolling harmlessly under her bench.

The message was clear, Mom was headhunting. She cranked up and zipped the second ball, only this time she overcorrected, and it went right, nearly taking out the cotton candy machine. The crowd gasped. Someone called her a crazy broad. Dad, hiding out near the stage, went searching for the source.

Winding up a third time, Cullen stuck out his hand, stepping forward. "Hang on, hang on. Mrs. Hawthorne. Can I give it a shot?"

Mom dropped her arm, bent at the elbow. She glanced at the dunk booth and shrugged. "Sure, I've got seventy-eight more tickets."

She stepped to the side. The crowd strained their necks to get a glimpse of the reliever. Mayor Pickens sized up Cullen and gave the worried spectators a smile. Cullen looked well out of place in his skater clothes, and besides, he appeared too small to do any real damage.

Cullen gripped the ball and smirked, spitting on the ground before wiping his mouth with his arm. He squinted at the target, dug in, and hurled a screaming fastball dead center.

Ping

The target snapped back. The chair squeaked as it dropped Mayor Pickens like a bag of ready mix into the murky waters.

Splash.

Another collective gasp from the crowd. Mom covered her

face. Someone shrieked as the mayor flailed and splashed like an overboard sailor during a storm. We inched closer as Old Pickens surfaced, hunched over in the waist high water and wiping at his face. With a lopsided smile, he waved to the stunned onlookers. But all eyes were back on Cullen, who stood juggling another baseball in his hand.

"Well, this kid's got an arm!" The mayor gurgled, wiping and spitting and trying to catch his breath. He was right about one thing, Cullen *did* have an arm. In all my time in the dugout, I'd never seen someone throw so hard.

"And he's got, oh, say, over two-hundred pitches left," Mom announced.

With assistance, the mayor made it back onto his seat, and for the next half hour all other attractions were abandoned. The donkeys took a nap. The horses were left to chew straw in peace, whipping their tails at the occasional fly. The Tilt-A-Whirl sat quietly unattended, and the concession stands were forgotten. Because everyone in the park was over at the dunking booth where Cullen nailed the bullseye over and over and over again.

Cullen pegged the lever so many times that it bent and dangled crookedly from its loosened bolt. Until two men in coveralls waved their hands in surrender and announced that the booth was out of order. Mayor Pickens, thoroughly pickled and out of breath, was given a fresh towel as someone went to hunt down his bifocals.

"But we've still got nine throws left," Mom said, standing beside Cullen with a hand on her hip.

"Well I'm sorry, miss, but this game is over," one of the guys in coveralls said, regarding my mom as though she were deranged. And that day, she kind of was.

Mayor Pickens adjusted his glasses, dripping wet and shell-shocked from the relentless drenching. Mom scrunched her nose as she turned to us. "Way to throw, Cullen."

"Wow, I didn't know you played baseball," I said as we made our way through the crowd.

Cullen gave me a casual shrug. "I don't."

The crowd thinned, whispering and pointing to Mom and Cullen as they drifted back toward the other games and tents set up near the creek. That's when Coach Peebles wandered over, brushing past me to get to Cullen. "Hey son, couldn't help but see you pitch over there, who you playing for?"

"Nobody," he said, and I watched as Coach Peebles' eyes lit up at the prospect of finding an ace free-agent.

"You don't play?" he said, unable to hide his widening smile. "Well, pitching like that, we sure could use you this afternoon. I got a jersey in the car, and..."

Cullen, hardly sweating, looked bored at the thought. "Nah, thanks though."

Coach Peebles eyed him suspiciously, tugging at his goatee. "Okay, well if you change your mind, you're more than welcome to play," he said before turning to me, suddenly remembering I existed. "You too, Marcus, you can both play in the double header if you want."

We laughed for a while about that, sitting with Mom at the picnic tables. Until Mayor Pickens approached, slumped over with a beach towel draped across his shoulders. He looked like a refugee who'd been rescued from flood waters. Mom studying him closely, nothing but warm satisfaction on her face.

The mayor nodded, his thinning hair still glistening in the sun.

"Mrs. Hawthorne," he said with a shiver. "I just wanted to thank you for your support. The Humane Society people are thrilled with this year's fundraising."

Mom shot him a smile so bright I needed my solar eclipse shoe box to face it head on. "Mayor Pickens, I assure you, the pleasure was entirely mine."

"Yes, well. Thank you," he said, then turning to Cullen and me, "And you, young man. That's quite an arm you have."

"Don't forget, you owe her nine throws," Cullen said. I stifled a laugh. Mr. Pickens' plastic smile melted a little as he jerked his head back to Mom.

"Why yes, of course. I'm sure we can work something out."

More political signs popped up around town. Mostly the blue, *Bush/Quale* signs, but some *Clinton/Gore* ones over near the college and downtown. I'd kept an eye open for a Ross Perot sign but those were scarce. I'd taken to pointing them out when we happened to pass one by on the road. Dad got a kick out of that. He said nobody would ever vote for a sleazy billionaire simply because he said what they wanted to hear.

Dad thought Perot would only gift wrap the election for Clinton, and then the country would be in big trouble. I asked him how much trouble, and he launched into a tirade about how Clinton had dodged the draft and didn't support our troops. That sounded bad, but when I asked Mom about the draft-dodging, she whipped around and said we had no business in Vietnam anyway. So you can see why I was so confused. To me, politics was like a glass prism, because no one saw it from the same angle.

But with the Republican Convention less than a week away, I thought maybe then I could get some answers to where the president stood on the issues. In the meantime, I asked Dad how if he voted for Bush, and Mom voted for Clinton, and Mrs. Tinkerton voted for Perot, wouldn't that sort of cancel things out? Dad looked at me with a grin and said he would be proud to cancel out Mom's vote. Those two, I'm telling you.

And things got cooking on Tuesday. With Dad at work, Cullen and I were in my room listening to the Beasties when an old Volkswagen pulled up slow on the street. We rushed out to find Mom in the living room.

"Oh good, they're here."

"Who's here?"

"Well," she said, with a hint of sneakiness, "I'm hosting a strategic planning committee."

"Sweet," Cullen said, but I think he meant the giant bowl of colorful salsa Mom had set out. Like me, I don't think he knew what a strategic planning committee was or did.

I opened the door, coming face to face with the old guy from the city council meeting. Mom introduced him as Mr. Earnest Bardwell. "Hello boys," he said, smiling at Cullen and me, his short white hair at ends with his suntanned face. And when he shook my hand, his firm grip was every bit as strong as his deep voice.

Our next visitor was not so charming. Ethan was a moody, long-haired jerk who wore ratty jeans and a gray jacket over a filthy yellow shirt even though it was summer and in the upper eighties. He smelled like an old gym class sneaker and didn't say much, only that he wanted to rip out that Bush/Quale sign in the yard and toss it to the street. I'd have liked to see him try. Dad would've made short work of Ethan.

After meeting Ethan, I was about to retreat to my room when a carload of college girls arrived right at my front doorstep —and forever changed my views on strategic planning committees. All shorts and t-shirts, they swept into the house smelling of flowers and fruit, announcing their plans to "Rock the Vote." The environment was their biggest concern, and Mom smiled proudly as they gushed about her editorials and how she'd stood up to an oppressive system.

Cullen and I exchanged smiles. Sure, whatever. Count us in.

Our meeting got underway in the living room. Mom read

from her notes. As of today, the ground-breaking ceremony was only a month away. Ethan sat on the floor, happy to be unhappy, his knees pulled to his chest as he rocked back and forth, mumbling his displeasure about *everything* until Mom dropped her notes to her waist, asking if he had something to add.

"So, how can you live in the same house as this man? The one who's building this...monstrosity of capitalism?"

Cullen turned to me and mouthed, *What?* I gave him my best smirk. Mom's eyes narrowed, locking in on her target. It was the kind of look I knew from experience was usually followed by serious punishment. She took a big breath. "Well, Ethan, first and foremost, that man you're talking about is my husband. And secondly, I do not fault the men and women doing the actual work. They are doing what they have to do to make a living. Lastly, I do not condemn capitalism; I condemn the proposed site of the store. My fight is with the corporation, period. Now if you want to insult my family, I will politely ask you to leave."

My mom could articulate her thoughts like a rapid-fire assault rifle. Cullen let out a low whistle. Ethan shifted but didn't move. His gaze fell to his knees and he muttered something under his breath. I could've warned him not to do that, had he asked.

"I'm sorry, did you have anything else?" Mom asked, leaning near and ready to finish him off. Ethan could only shake his head. One of the girls giggled.

"Good. So, okay, here's what I think we should do. I had some flyers printed. I'd like to post them at every corner, at the drugstore, at the college campuses, the nearby malls, wherever they can be seen. The biggest advantage we have is our voices, we need to get the word out."

"We can post them at the park," Cullen said, reaching for a few of the flyers. I squirmed. So far I'd been able to balance on a tightrope of neutrality. But now Mom had gone and had flyers made, and before I even had a chance to read them she was handing over a stack to Cullen. He stood, ready to go, waiting on me. I sat paralyzed, torn between loyalties, wondering how in the world Switzerland managed to stay out of these sticky situations. Then, like gripping the knife that would find my dad's back, I snatched the staple gun from the coffee table and followed Cullen out the door.

We hopped on our bikes, headed for Wilson Road. Once again, I tried to keep up with Cullen, but even on that rickety bike he was too fast. The wind blew through his hair as he climbed the hills with ease until we hit the sidewalks. He skidded to a stop and slapped a flyer on the post and then with a few clicks of staples we were off. I watched each passing car, just waiting to see Dad's truck.

We arrived at Squabble Creek ten minutes later, coasting around the steep bends and blind curves. I prayed a tractor trailer didn't come by and flatten us like flies on a windshield. Cullen slowed, pointing past the cemetery where two pickup trucks were parked. He came to a halt behind a tree.

"I should go flatten their tires," Cullen said, hardly winded. I was gasping for breath so hard I could only shake my head, unable to articulate what a bad idea it was. I mean, the meeting thing was fun, but this seemed dangerous.

A crew of surveyors stood around a tripod, too close to the truck. I turned to whisper again that we should bolt, but he was off, coasting a little ways toward the truck, ditching his bike in the thickets behind a tree.

"Cullen!" I called out. It was no use. Without turning back, he motioned for me to follow, and I did of course, because I had the backbone of toilet tissue.

The workers weren't doing much other than standing around smoking cigarettes. I set my bike with Cullen's and crawled over to him, which didn't make much sense but made me feel less visible.

"What are you doing?" I asked, risking a peek. We were close enough to hear parts of their conversations, laughing and grunting and something about a waitress at Della's Diner. Cullen leaned in close enough I could study the chip in one of his front teeth.

"I'm going to let the air out of the tires in the truck."

"What? I thought you were joking!"

"Just on the side facing us," he continued, like it was no big thing. A roar of terror shimmied down my spine. Yet, stupid as this plan was, I felt myself nodding along. Part of me figured, why not? It wasn't like I could change his mind.

The men were maybe twenty yards away—two first-downs on a football field. The truck was only one first-down away.

"Stay here and take watch," he whispered, giving me an out. His eyes darted wildly, from the truck back to me. "If they look toward the truck, just hoot like an owl then take off. Don't worry about me, I'll get away."

He turned and slunk off before I could tell him how lately my voice was on the fritz, so I wasn't quite sure how exactly my owl hoots might sound. It wasn't like I could practice. I spied the crew again, feeling a little like Rambo. Cullen crouched low, then dashed like a gazelle, hopping nimbly over a downed tree limb before rolling to a stop behind the truck. He smiled at me just as the workers broke into another round of laughter.

I don't think this was what Mom had in mind when she let us leave with the staple gun, now lying on the ground near our bikes, glinting in the sun. But right then, I didn't know which parent to trust or who was right. I only knew that if we got caught doing this my dad would skip punishment and actually kill me. After he disowned me.

I watched in horror as Cullen reached into his pocket and

pulled out a knife. My heart nearly took me for a ride. I was about to run to my bike and high tail it out of there when, instead of stabbing the tire, he gently placed it into the stem and gave me a thumbs up. The workers were now actually looking into the tripod thing. Then I glanced back to Cullen, behind the tire. From where I was it appeared like nothing was happening. But after a few torturous minutes the truck sat on its rim.

Cullen pointed toward the men and I checked, counting five. Then I flashed a shaky thumbs-up and Cullen scurried to the front.

Again he placed the blade of the knife on the stem, the tire hissing as one of the men laughed and whooped then started hacking. He pounded his chest and coughed again. Then he started for the truck.

"Hoot Hoot Hoot!"

My hoots sounded more like a donkey braying. But this was no time for style points. Cullen jerked the knife away and glanced under the truck where a couple of guys were rounding the front of the truck. He started to retreat to the back but coughing man was at the tailgate. I hooted again, just as the man lowered the tailgate and took notice of the flattened back tire.

I blinked hard, until sparks of fear flashed across my eyelids like a meteor shower. My knees jammed, locked in place. All I could do was watch as the others came around to inspect the front tires. At the last second, Cullen rolled under the truck.

The coughing man called for the others. "Hey Andy, ya'll come take a look at this."

Then all five of them were at the truck, rubbing their bellies and considering the mystery.

"Did you run over some glass?" one of them asked.

"I don't think so. Must have been a nail again." Andy sighed heavily as he knelt, taking a closer look at the tires.

Trying to get myself together, I was about to throw a stick in the brush or yell out for a distraction when Cullen slipped out from the other side.

He was like a ninja, the way he popped out from under the truck. I held my breath, waiting for one of the dunces to see him. When they didn't, he slithered from between the two vehicles, paused to listen, then dashed off toward the woods. It was amazing, but I didn't have much time to enjoy it because at once the crew all looked up toward me.

I hit the ground like a sack. I held my breath and kept as still as possible. I counted to sixty, thinking, *I'm sorry, Dad, I'm sorry I got you fired today.* Then I kept right on counting to a hundred just to be safe. When I still didn't hear footsteps, I slowly raised my head and found the crew piling into the other truck. Andy tossed his Coke can to the ground and shut the door, and the other truck cranked up.

I exhaled a huge sigh of relief, seconds before I realized they were about to drive right past me.

We dropped our bikes on the front lawn and booked it inside. Once we were safely in my room, I started pacing. Wringing my hands, I turned to Cullen, shaking my head. "I'm out. No more for me. Do you know what would happen to me if my dad found out I was flattening tires at the site?"

"Relax," Cullen said, falling into my beanbag chair. He was still brimming with adrenaline, his dark eyes danced with his smile. "It was just a prank."

"A prank? Are you crazy?" My voice quivered. My whole body shook. I dropped to my bed and took a deep breath, my thoughts all jangled up from the fear and the heat. I could still hear the truck crunching up the gravel road, right after I'd miraculously dove into the brush with the bikes, surely collecting a new army of chiggers along the way.

"That was way too close. And I can't believe you flattened the other two tires after they left."

"Ha! That was the best part of the whole thing." Cullen clasped his hands behind his head. "Man, I wish I could see their faces when they come back." He shot upright. "Hey, should we go see?"

"No!" I shook my head. "Seriously, Cullen, I don't want to do this again."

He looked me over, his smile masquerading as concern. Then he nodded his head. "Okay, then. We won't." Then he reached around to his back pocket and produced the rest of the crumpled flyers. "But I still have to post these."

Mom invited Cullen to stay for dinner, but he had things to do around his house. After our little brush with death it was probably for the best that he didn't, I don't think I could handle being around him and my dad at the same time.

Dinner that evening was stuffed peppers, an alien-like merger of meat and vegetables. Judging by the bang-blowing gusty sigh Dad let out as he took his seat, I don't think he was thrilled about it either. Nevertheless, he dished out a pepper.

"So, a funny thing happened at the job site today."

I swallowed down a golf ball-sized lump of worry. Dad let the steam rise from the innards of the green carcass sitting on his plate. "We had Larry and a crew of guys out there doing some surveying, last-minute prep stuff before we break ground, and uh, well the truck tires were flattened."

Mom's eyes widened with surprise. I locked my gaze on the main dish, wondering whether this rubbery pepper thing would be my last meal. What a terrible way to go.

"Yeah, just flattened, not slashed or anything. There was no damage, well, if you don't count the two hours lost for us to get out there with an air compressor," Dad continued as I got my affairs in order. "Sounds like something a couple of kids would do, doesn't it, Marcus?"

Slap went the pepper on my plate. *Marcus? No, Marcus doesn't speak English. He's on strike. I'm sorry, what was the question?* I bought some time with a cough before forcing my head to nod "Um, I guess."

Dad grimaced. "Well, maybe you could keep your ears perked," he said, looking back toward the door. "Weren't you with that Cullen kid all day?"

Define "all day." I wasn't with him this morning at breakfast. Or now. Was Cullen a suspect? Had the crew seen him? Was this a test? Was I an accomplice? A mudslide of sweat washed down my back. Thankfully Mom spoke, because I was about to start hooting again.

"Yes, in fact they were right here most of the day, weren't you, Marcus?"

"Most of the day?" Dad asked, one eyebrow raised. He sipped his milk then leveled his eyes on me. "Because I don't trust that kid one bit, he's got trouble written all over his face. And his dad, what does he even do?"

"What does *that* have to do with anything?" Mom asked, her eyes hardening. Dad retreated a little.

"I'm just saying, I don't exactly see his dad going to work every morning."

"He's fixing up the house," I said, scooping a spoonful of brown rice onto my plate. "I mean, that's what Cullen said, that they were staying there and fixing up the place." I tried to sound casual, but my voice came out like a Girl Scout.

Dad wasn't buying it. "Oh, well I haven't seen him swinging a hammer or drill or anything, either."

Mom tilted her head. "I don't think it's right for us to sit here and judge people we don't know. Our own neighbors at that."

Here we go, I thought. Dad took a weary breath and tried to soothe things. "Look, I'm not judging, I'm just...I don't know, it's been a hectic day, and we don't need vandals or kids messing things up," he said, and I thought things might settle some until he added, "I'm only asking because I saw your flyers."

Mom blanched. "My uh," she coughed a few times and then pulled it together. "My flyers?"

Dad's shoulders fell. "Ana, who else would make up those flyers? 'Save the Cemetery, preserve your history.' You may as well have posted your picture."

It was a rare moment when my mom went speechless. We ate in silence for a minute then Dad smiled at her. With my fork, I scooted around the wilted pepper and nibbled on the rice. When Dad spoke again his voice was softer. "Hon," he said, reaching for her arm. "What do you expect me to do? I mean, the whole thing with the mayor, and now you're posting flyers and organizing a protest. Please, tell me what you think it is I should do?"

Mom struggled to muffle her small giggle when he mentioned the mayor. The day after the dunking booth, *The Bugle* had run a picture of the water-logged mayor on the front page. It was tacked up on the fridge, so every morning I found myself looking right into Mayor Pickens' dizzy eyes. But this time Dad wasn't being funny, he was pleading.

Ever since Mega More announced their plans these moments had become all too common, and I wasn't sure how long we could go on like this. At that moment, I really hated Mega More.

Mom took a moment to gather her thoughts, rubbing my dad's hand. "Ben, I don't know. I can't tell you what you should do, but I need to do what I think is right, you know that. You could always go back to school, do side jobs. We could get by."

Dad's face tightened. The way they stared at each other it was like I wasn't in the room. They weren't yelling or loud, and in a way that was even worse. Dad's voice was serious. "Honey, I've worked so hard to get to where I am, and you're asking me to walk away from the biggest job of my life. I can't do that."

Mom nodded. "And I can't just do *nothing*."

It felt like they were on the brink of something. Like everything hinged on what he'd do next. I sat at the table, my hand gripping my fork. The steaming pepper on my plate. Then Dad drew a breath and looked at my mom with eyes that held so much love I thought he might fall over.

"I knew that on the day I married you."

A swirl of relief blew over the room. Mom smiled back at

him. "Yet you still went through with it." She leaned closer and kissed him on the cheek.

"Hey, no kissing at the table," I reminded them.

Dad smiled at me then turned back to Mom playfully. "Well okay, so that's how it's going to be, huh? But I want you to know that in our home you're my wife, but out there," he pointed to the door, "we're sworn enemies. And don't expect me to go easy on you."

Mom jerked her hand back with a smile. "Or I on you."

And with that, I took a big old bite of the alien-like carcass, happy I'd live to see another day.

After the prank down at Squabble Creek, I was ready to steer my summer back on track. So when Danny called and asked me to come out for baseball practice at ten the next morning, I jumped at the chance.

Having already missed the first few games, I showed up ready to resume my position as bench warmer extraordinaire. But when I stepped into the dugout, it wasn't Danny who greeted me but Coach Peebles.

He stood, adjusting his dusty baseball cap. "Well, there he is, our long-lost Pirate. Where ya been, Hawthorne?"

I shrugged, flattening tires to halt the construction of the Mega More didn't strike me as the best answer. Before I could grunt out much of anything, he sent me off to fill the water cooler. Hmm, maybe this was some sort of punishment. I would have to earn my way back onto the team.

It was sweltering hot already, but it was nice, getting back out there. The smell of the grass, the familiar *tink* of aluminum bats, the squeak of the wagon wheels as I hauled the sloshing cooler full of hose water back to the dugout. When I returned, Coach Peebles clapped my shoulder as Danny took the mound.

"Well, it's good to have you around again," he said and then pointed toward the outfield. "Some of the guys are running late, you want to take left field?"

"Sure." I turned for my glove.

Coach cleared his throat and held me back before I stormed

the field. "So uh, I was sort of hoping you could talk that friend of yours into playing. What's his name again?"

"Cullen," I answered, my shoulders sagging. How had I not seen this coming? Coach didn't want me. He only wanted Cullen. What was I thinking? Just that fast, I wanted to be kicking a skateboard down the street to his house, not here, being used as a recruiter.

Coach Peebles called out to Danny, something about his release. He spit, mixed the sludge of juice into the red sand with his foot, then shot me a wink. "Well, we sure could use him."

"Yeah, sure, I'll talk to him."

I spent the next hour in the outfield, studying the grass or looking at the sky, sweating and swatting mosquitoes while thinking about Mom and Dad and the Mega More. Only once did a ball come my way, soggy from a roll in the grass. I scooped it up and made a wobbly throw to second.

After practice, Coach Peebles treated Danny and me to lunch at McDonalds. But even that wasn't worth the hassle, because as soon as we sat down with my super-sized Patrick Ewing Olympic cup (I wanted the Michael Jordan cup, but it was never in stock), Coach Peebles started in on me. "So, your mom still at it with the protesting and stuff?" he said, digging into his french fries.

I nodded, jamming salty fries into my mouth to buy time. Coach Peebles stared on, Danny like his clone as they talked and laughed about practice. Above their heads, one of Mom's protest posters was still taped up on the glass. I smiled, remembering the manager chasing us off as we plastered the building with the flyers. I guess he missed one.

Eventually, things turned to Mega More, which meant Danny asking if I'd talked some sense into my mom. I told him there wasn't much she could do anymore, trying to remain neutral with a vague answer.

"Good, because do you know how much Pepsi will go to a Mega More?" Coach Peebles said, and I guessed that it was a rhetorical question. Danny glanced up from his quarter pounder.

"But is it true that they're going to pave over the cemetery?" he said, looking to his dad. Coach Peebles groaned.

"Come on, Danny, you're not letting this stuff get in your head, are you? That little cemetery won't be harmed, and it can sit there like it always has, safe and sound."

"Well, the store says the cemetery will not be harmed, but there may be more graves, closer to the site. At least that's what the historical society says." The words spilled out of my mouth before I could stop myself.

Coach Peebles looked at me like I had slugs coming out of my ears. He stabbed at the ice in his drink with his straw. "Marcus, your mom can feed you all of this stuff about saving the Earth, but that store is going to save this *town*," he said in a way that ended the conversation. I sipped my drink, feeling the burn of the soda. A few drops of rain hit the window and Coach Peebles scurried out to put the windows up in his truck. Danny scooped up a fry and started talking baseball again, but I'd decided that was it for me. I didn't want to tag along this season.

I didn't want last summer. I wanted this summer.

The rain came in heavy all afternoon, so when Dad got home he had to peel off his muddy boots, strip down, and make a run for the shower, which was good because I was still having trouble looking him in the eye after the whole Squabble Creek incident.

I'd only just confessed it all to Mom before he arrived, thinking it might help to get it off my chest. Part of me thought she'd be happy—we were only trying to help, after all—but when I got to the stuff about Cullen letting the air out of the tires, rolling under the truck, our narrow escape, her eyes went as big as baseballs. I guess I got caught up in the story and totally forgot it was my mom sitting there, not some partner in crime. And when she told me to take a seat and started pacing around like she did when she was thinking, I knew I'd messed up.

"I don't want you going back to the site without me," she said sternly. I nodded. Her voice carried a worry that matched her eyes. "I'm serious, Marcus. It's not safe, and I don't want you in any kind of trouble."

"Okay, Mom," I said. She only stared at the floor. "We were just trying to help."

She stopped suddenly and brought a hand to her mouth. I knew I'd messed up then—it wasn't easy to shock my mother like that. Eventually she nodded, slowly. "Honey, as much as I don't want the store there, I don't want you...I... This is not what I wanted."

And that's when Dad pulled up.

Now, as Dad was freshly showered and whistling, raring to go with the Republican Convention set to get underway, we sat down for dinner.

Mom seemed to have pulled herself together, because she was humming and singing her own tune as she put on a mitt and removed some sort of casserole from the depths of the oven. Dad gave me a funny look, and I caught a whiff of something awful. She set the dish in the middle of the table, and we both instinctively leaned away from the toxic steam radiating from whatever was hiding under a blanket of golden cheese.

"Who's ready for some broccoli casserole?"

There wasn't enough cheese in the world to make something as despicable as broccoli go down without a fight, and judging by Dad's crinkly nose, he agreed. I looked around for a side dish, bread or potatoes, anything to help with the effort. But it was no use. The main dish was riding solo.

Mom scooped out a miserable block of the stuff. The green sprouts and stems poking out made my stomach turn.

"Yum," Dad said in a way that made clear that this was not "yum" at all. Mom smiled just a little too hard.

"Well, I was thinking, you know how President Bush hates broccoli? Well, I made this in his honor."

With Mom up to her old tricks again, I was the one paying the price. On my plate I went for the cheese, stripping down the casserole like a puzzle. After the cheese, I went for the noodles, occasionally finding a bit of the beast in my mouth. I choked down some milk and went back on the hunt.

"So, what time do the lies start?" Mom said, referring to the convention.

Dad set down his napkin, like a boxer throwing in the towel. "Okay now, I was good for your little hug fest, so you have to return the favor."

"You're right, honey," she said, batting her eyelashes. "What time does the convention start?"

"Eight 'o clock, and I'm asking you to be on good behavior. Show some respect for the president."

Mom's eyes closed to squints. I could tell her tongue was thrashing around inside her mouth, clenched by her teeth to keep it in check. If nothing else, tonight was going to be interesting.

The Republican Convention kicked off exactly like the Democratic Convention: Red, white, and blue everywhere, stars, and the crowd cheering wildly with signs and funny hats, looking like they were at the Super Bowl.

Tom Brokaw welcomed us to Houston, Texas. In the background, down on the stage, some old guy hammered away from the podium. Mr. Brokaw stressed how tonight would be the most important speech of President Bush's life. Clinton still had a lead, but the President was surging. I thought back to

Governor Clinton and his passionate speech at the Democratic Convention. It would be tough to beat.

After a commercial break, which Mom spent gloating about Mr. Clinton's lead; the network did a piece on Vice President Dan Quayle and all the funny things he said. Dad grimaced, and I thought Mom was going to turn purple she was having such a hard time holding back.

When former President Reagan took the stage to speak, his familiar voice was gentle and soothing as he lauded the American Century and Model-T Fords and Empire of Ideals. Dad's eyes shined as his hero spoke, while Mom's glare hardened when he talked about cleaning house in the Senate. I took a break to find a snack in the kitchen because I could still taste broccoli in my mouth. I had to admit, I was with the prez on that one.

Next up was the main event, although judging by the crowd, Ronald Reagan had stolen the show. President Bush gripped the podium and Mom sat back with a smirk. Dad leaned forward to listen.

With his comforting, grandfather-like tone, I came away feeling like President Bush genuinely cared about the country and its history. He spoke earnestly about the Berlin Wall, the fall of the Soviets, how the Arabs and the Israelis were at peace.

I didn't know much about politics, but so far it seemed like Bill Clinton painted a picture of change while the president presented a collage of the past. Where Bush seemed blind to the hard times some people were going through, Clinton seemed compassionate and willing to help.

But what did I know?

For me it was as confusing as the whole Mega More debate. Jobs would come with the store, but at what cost? How do we keep the past and change the future? How could both be right? What was the right answer? Was there even an answer at all?

Was it like math where you had to find the correct answer, or would more than one way get us where we needed to go? My head started to hurt just thinking about it.

I wandered off to bed as Mom and Dad geared up their debate. I was too confused to ask questions only to be more confused by their conflicting answers. If the truth was somewhere in the middle, as Mr. Howell often said, didn't that mean both these guys were lying?

I didn't get much time to myself at home, so when Mom ran up to the grocery store and left me alone for twenty minutes, I took full advantage of the opportunity. I blasted the Beasties on our home stereo, testing the limits of Dad's tall Sony speakers. The mirror shook on the wall as I rapped along, bouncing from the couch to the chair, imagining I was the fourth Beastie Boy, until I saw something move from the corner of my eye.

I screamed when I saw Cullen, who had joined in, stomping around the living room just as I jumped off the couch. Scrambling for the stereo, my cheeks burned hot as I smacked at the buttons until the room went silent.

"Dude, nice moves," Cullen said, sliding a hand over his jagged hair, the sides of which had been shaved. In his other hand he had a grease stained bag.

"Breakfast?" he asked, shoving a biscuit in my face. "Two for a buck."

I took a quick scan of the driveway for the Renault. We'd have to hide the evidence and maybe open a window to air out the fumes. Cullen tore off a bite of his breakfast, his eyes brightening as he chewed. I took another glance at the spotted bag.

"Sure."

I tore into my biscuit as Cullen mumbled through a mouthful. "Oh, I need your help."

"My help?"

"Yeah, remember the grass? At the Pettyjohn's?" he said. "I was thinking I could do the front and you do the back. We can split the twenty-five bucks. Well, thirteen for me and twelve for you."

"Why do I only get twelve? The back is bigger."

He put his arm around me. "Call it a finder's fee. Besides, you know you want to go down there and stare at your old babysitter."

"She's not—forget it."

I changed clothes and found my old Nike's—the ones with the grass stained soles that were splitting at the toe. Cullen hopped up from the stoop when I came outside.

"Oh uh, we need gas too," he said. I ran down and hauled up the canister from the basement. I wrote a quick note for Mom, then, returning to the front yard, ready to get moving, Cullen shrugged with a smile. "And your mower?"

"You don't have a mower?"

"Ours is in the shop."

And it was with my mower and my gas, that we headed down the street to cut the grass at a thirteen/twelve "split." Then again, it wasn't like I was doing anything important. My dance moves could wait.

Even with a sky full of clouds, it was already muggy out. I was thinking about going back for the bug spray when Cullen stopped in front of his house. "Hang on, I've got to run in and grab something," he said, without inviting me in.

The Buick wasn't in the driveway, only a thick, oval oil stain. I pulled the mower to the curb and stared at the house.

Since the Ramsey's had left the neighborhood, the wooden siding on the house had rippled and warped as it turned green with the mildew working its way to the windows. I figured

Cullen's dad would get to the outside of the house whenever he finished fixing up the inside.

With Cullen taking forever, it wasn't long before I grew bored staring at all the junk laying around in the splotchy yard. The wooden fence posts were soft, the railings sagging in some places and broken in others. Some trash lay near the rotted woodpile at the side of the house where an entanglement of vines and thicket of thorns climbed up a knotty old maple that was only a wind gust away from falling right onto the patchy roof.

I crept to the porch, gently tapping on the old screen door hanging open. "Hey Cullen?"

Inside, the house was completely still. I glanced back to the empty driveway, then opened the creaky door and stuck my head in.

"Cullen," I said again, catching a whiff of something awful. A powerful stench like something was rotting in there. I set my shirt over my nose and called for him again, but the words caught in my throat. Not much furniture, piles of clothes and bulging trash bags. The wallpaper was curled and torn, hanging as it peeled along the vents. The Ramsey's old television sat on a table under the window, ashtrays overflowing with butts onto the matted carpet that held spots and stains where it wasn't covered with trash.

I could only stare at the mess. On the dining room table sat two or three pizza boxes and plates, cups, half empty glasses of soda. Lots of beer bottles. I swallowed hard, turning to leave when the toilet flushed upstairs just before Cullen's feet hit the steps. He stopped when he saw me.

"Dude, what are you doing? I told you to wait outside."

There was a flash of anger I hadn't heard from him before. I shook my head, backing out of the door and out into the welcoming sticky air. I took a deep breath. Cullen stepped out on the porch behind me, slamming the door shut, his Vans tied together and strewn over his shoulder.

Walking to the Pettyjohn's, he didn't say anything for a while, and I had no idea what to say to him. I'd only been in the Ramsey's house once, a couple of years ago with Mom when they had an estate sale. Sifting through their stuff, the floors shined with polish and the rooms sparkled and smelled of lemon and oil soap. Mr. Ramsey used to keep the yard like a putting green. Like I said, Dad thought it was a shame how the house was left to sit empty and rot.

Whatever Cullen's father was doing at the house, it surely wasn't renovating. I couldn't imagine what Dad would do if he saw what I'd just seen. I was still thinking about that when Cullen looked up, the easy-going smile returning to his face. "So uh, our cleaning lady's been on strike," he laughed, tying up a shoe. I tried to laugh, but the house had sucked the life out of me.

"Uh, your dad's fixing up the house, right?"

"Yeah," he said, only it was more of a desperate laugh than his usual joking laugh. "Right. Come on."

We filled the mower with gas. I stood around on the walkway as Cullen mowed the front yard. Thankfully, there was no sign of Caitlyn, but the day was heating up and I couldn't help but notice that there was a whole lot more shade in the front yard than the in the back.

When it was my turn to cut the sun beaten, much bigger backyard, I glanced up to the back of Caitlyn's house, thinking back two years ago when she was my sitter. She spent most of her time on the phone and letting me do whatever I pleased, and it was a nice arrangement we had, until one night when she had her boyfriend over and Mom and Dad just so happened to come home early. That was it for Caitlyn, and to this day she thinks I ratted her out.

I was slogging my way down the backyard hill when I ran out of gas. I rounded the house for the canister, where I found Cullen on the porch swing, shooting the breeze with none other than Caitlyn Pettyjohn and a friend. Judging by the bikini tops and towels, the girls looked to be headed for the pool.

"Oh, there you are," Cullen said, as though I'd been lost. Yep, there I was all right, sweating through my shirt, covered in grass and dirt, and doing most of the work.

Caitlyn cut her eyes at me. Sort of amazing how long she could hold a grudge. She sighed, tossed her towel around her neck and called after her mom. For someone so pretty she could shoot a stare to freeze a fire.

Mrs. Pettyjohn rushed out the door without noticing us. "Okay, let's move it girls."

They waved to Cullen as they climbed into the van, Caitlyn flung her hair back, sending me one last glare before she shut the door. With the radio blaring they started up the road for the pool, leaving Cullen and me to deal with the heat. I grabbed the gas container and grumbled. "So, you really got the better end of this deal," I said, turning to head around back.

"Hey," he jumped up. "My bad. I didn't know that the backyard was so big. Tell you what. Let me finish up."

"Seriously?"

"Yeah, sure. I like cutting grass, besides, you look like you could use a break." He pointed to a cup of ice water on the wicker table. "Caitlyn thought I might be thirsty," he said with a smile that put Tom Sawyer to shame.

"Um, okay," I said, still not able to tell if he was serious. But he was serious. I sat back on the porch, sipping ice water and trying to enjoy the breeze while Cullen finished up the backyard but instead feeling guilty for letting him do all the work.

But that was Cullen. Just when it seemed like he was

conning me into something, he'd flash a smile and I'd forget the whole thing. He was unpredictable and fun. I never knew what sort of stunts he would come up with, good or bad. But I always looked forward to finding out.

Lugging the mower up the street, I asked if he wanted to use it to cut his yard.

"Nah, I think that's enough with the grass today. Oh, here," he said, handing me a five. "She only gave me a twenty and a five, I'll have to get change."

I stuffed the bill in my pocket. Something told me five bucks was all that was coming my way. But then again, he had done most of the cutting. Besides, after seeing the inside of his house, he needed the cash more than I did.

Cullen stopped suddenly. He slapped my arm and pointed up to my house. "Dude, it's Mr. Bardwell."

Sure enough, the ancient Beetle sat halfway off the road, parked crookedly on the curb. My heart kicked up a notch, because if Mr. Bardwell was there, it meant another strategic planning meeting. And another strategic planning meeting meant a car full of college girls was on the way over to my house.

S trategic Planning Meeting number two was a bust. Only Mr. Bardwell showed. Cullen and I crashed on the couch, munching on granola bars while Mom and Mr. B talked about *Newsweek*. It was kind of a big deal though, Mom's piece. Mr. Carraway with *The Bugle* had contacted her about doing a story on her and Dad. Dad had already flat out refused, but Mom had his card and seemed to be mulling it over.

We slunk off, back to my room, where we cranked up the Beastie Boys and I flipped on the Nintendo. It was funny because Cullen was even worse than I was at video games, probably because he couldn't pay attention for more than a few seconds at a time.

I was up 37-7 in *Super Tecmo Bowl* and running wild with Bo Jackson after I'd broken the unspoken rule and selected the Los Angeles Raiders. When I scored yet again, I wiped the bangs out of my face to better gloat when Cullen, unfazed by the thrashing he was taking on the field, motioned to my head and said, "You should let me cut your hair."

"Yeah, right," I said, still on high alert after the chigger incident.

He shrugged, but a few minutes later he glanced over at me again, right in the middle of a play, too. I sacked Dan Marino and the ball squirted loose. My computer man scooped it up and took it the other way. Touchdown! I started dancing but Cullen hadn't even noticed.

"I'm serious. I've got clippers at my house. I do my hair," he said, sifting a hand over his head. Computer Howie Long celebrated in the end zone. I peeked over at Cullen, his hair was sort of longish on top and shaved around the sides. It did look cool, though. Mostly even, too. But still, chiggers.

"Come on." He jumped up. "Let's do it!"

"I don't know," I said, already feeling myself being lulled under his spell.

"I'll be right back." He darted out of the room. I kicked the extra point, making it 51-7.

Cullen returned in less than five minutes, knocking at the front door. Some muffled voices, then a few jaunty footsteps and he was back. From his pocket he produced the clippers. "Well, you ready?"

I took a breath. "I guess. I don't want it real short though. I have a weird shaped head."

"No arguing that. But look," he said, still pulling things out of his pockets. "I've got different guards." He placed the biggest one over the clippers, which were huge with massive teeth and a thick cord that was a mile long.

"Okay, let's do it in the bathroom," I said, because I was an agreeable sap.

We snuck across the hall toward the bathroom. Mom and Mr. Bardwell were discussing something about a protest in the kitchen. *Protest what?* I thought. The Mega More decision had already been made. Twice.

Cullen pushed me forward and we shut the door. He wasted no time plugging in the clippers, he yanked a towel off the shelf and tossed it over my shoulders like he was Vidal Sassoon. I sat on the toilet, eyeing him closely as he adjusted the guard.

I jumped when he fired up the clippers. "Dude, just chill."

Chill. As the clippers chattered along, growling like

Hannibal at the mailman. I could feel the powerful buzz vibrating in the floor. Cullen only smiled.

"Okay, I'm going to go across the top, don't make any sudden movements, got it?" he said, which did not help me chill.

Before I could say another word, the clippers tore into my hair like a paper shredder, ripping and tearing and leaving a trail down my scalp. Clumps of brown hair fell to my lap, on the sink, my shoes, everywhere. I managed to hold up my hand.

"Feels kinda short," I said, and Cullen stopped for a moment.

He shrugged. "Hmm. It's a little shorter than I thought."

"What?" I tried to hop up but Cullen set me back down.

"You gotta stay still." He took another buzzing swipe through my hair. To my horror, I reached up and felt only a prickly fuzz over my scalp.

"I thought you said it wouldn't be short?" I bolted up to look in the mirror. Yawee! All I saw was a mouth-breathing freak.

I must have screamed, or shrieked, or it could've been all the stuff I knocked over, but it wasn't long before footsteps rushed down the hall. The clippers buzzed angrily, hungry for more, when the door swung open.

"What in the wor—" Mom's hand flew to her mouth, but the hand did little to cover her laughter. Not a *laughing with you* kind of laugh, either. It didn't help how Cullen was already howling—even harder than he'd laughed when he was slathering pickle juice and mayonnaise on my legs.

Cullen shut the clippers off just as Mr. Bardwell joined the fun. "Now that's a haircut," he bellowed from the door. Mom shrieked again with laughter and I rolled my eyes. Who knew the old man was such a comedian? I summoned the courage for another peek at the mirror. It was sort of like a reverse Mohawk. The top of my head was shaved clean, leaving two curtains of hair on the sides. My first thought was Bozo the Clown.

"You were supposed to just trim it." I turned my head to Cullen, my gaze clinging to the idiot in the mirror.

"Here, let me even it out," Cullen said, cranking the clippers up and coming at me again before Mom swooped in and gently took them from his hand.

"Here, why don't you let *me* fix it?"

But there was no fixing it. All she could do was take the rest of the hair off to match. And that's what she did. I closed my eyes as I was sheared like a sheep. Cullen and Mr. Bardwell crowded the bathroom, giggling and joking about how they should collect my hair and sell it at an auction.

I sat as still as I could, surrendering to the hack job as Mom took the guard off and carefully trimmed around my ears, holding my head in place like she'd done when she'd wipe my face clean before letting me go to the bus stop when I was little.

"Okay, I think that's the best we can do," she said, finally turning off the shears but not the buzzing in my ears. Standing up, I looked in the mirror. I was bald, just some fuzz to cover my scalp.

"I guess you won't need a haircut for a while," Mom said, tapping the clippers on the sink.

"I look like an alien."

"It's not so terrible." Cullen tilted his head to one side as he inspected my scalp. "Besides, it will grow out by the time school starts."

"School! It will grow by then, right?" I said, counting the days in my head. My shoulders sagged and Mom ran a hand over my scalp.

"It feels kind of neat. Prickly."

"Oh, good. My head feels *neat*," I said.

"Like a chia pet. One that you just planted," Mom said. "Now we add water and wait."

I glared her. The problem with being a living, breathing

punchline is the whole getting punched part. And my gut had had about all it could take. And I was about to stomp and yell and throw a fit when Cullen stepped closer, picked up the clippers, and like the mowing thing he surprised me once again.

"Tell you what. I'll let you shave my head to make it even."

"What?" I should've been upset with him but it was impossible. It was like he had this force field of likeableness around him. Even as he'd just destroyed my hair, I felt a smile creeping across my face.

"You don't have to," I said, but he shrugged and clicked on the clippers. Mom stepped back.

"No, it's only fair. Watch out," he shouted over the buzz of the clippers. He took a seat on the toilet and handed them to me. "Okay, have at it."

The clippers were still warm from eating my hair. I looked to Mom, who asked Cullen what his parents would say.

"My old man won't care either way." Then, under his breath, "He probably won't even notice."

Mom's eyes widened with pity. But I knew Cullen didn't want that, so I set the trembling clippers to his head, wondering where to begin with his sandy blond curls, when he snagged them from my grip and tore right in. Pretty soon his yellow locks had joined the carnage of my brown ones on the floor.

"Oh, this is too much," Mr. Bardwell said with a wave. "Ana, you have fun, I'll see you next week and get back to you on what we discussed."

"Okay. Thank you, Earnest," Mom said, laughing. Then we watched as Cullen took the rest of his hair off.

WE WEREN'T EXACTLY TWINS. Cullen's head was round and smooth, and he was able to kind of pull it off in his own skater-dude kind of way. In fact, he hardly even looked different without hair.

Then there was me. I resembled a bald monkey, well, a bald monkey who'd been crossed with an alien and then bumped his head on its cage when he fell out of his traveling carnival wagon. Something like that.

It wasn't quite shaved but buzzed to where you could see the scar on the side of my head where I hit the coffee table a few years back while doing indoor somersaults. Plus, my head was misshapen. My ears were like open car doors. I pulled on a winter stocking cap and Mom put a broom in my hands and told me to clean up.

We were finishing up when Dad slammed through the front door, griping about work. "So get this. The ground breaking ceremony is only a few weeks away and Hank just quit on—"

He stopped midsentence when he saw us, his face somewhere between fear and laughter. "What in the world is going on in this house?"

Mom appeared in the doorway from the kitchen. "Well, let's see. Marcus wanted a haircut but didn't want to go to the salon. So, Cullen here brought over some clippers and, well..." she waved a hand over our heads. "Marcus, show your father."

I took off my hat.

He openly winced, then tried to recover. "A trim, huh?"

"It'll grow back," Mom said, waving him off.

Dad stared at us for a hard minute. Then he took a deep sigh and shook his head, walking down the hallway toward his room. Mom winked at us.

"We're so punk rock," Cullen said.

Oh, we were something all right.

A recap of the past few weeks:

- Mom and Dad called a truce with the yard signs, agreeing to keep one each, equal sized, Bush and Clinton signs at opposite ends of the yard.
- Cullen and I sat in the stands at one of Danny's baseball games at the park and ended up with matching sunburns on our heads (Coach Peebles was still begging Cullen to play).
- Mom did the interview with Mr. Carraway at *The Bugle* and continued to openly trash the mayor.
- Mayor Pickens fired back with his own interview in which he called Mom a loose cannon (Mom was flattered).
- Cullen tried to teach me how to do a McTwist on the Gator but I fell and earned myself a cantaloupe-sized bruise on my left butt cheek (Mom wasn't happy).
- Mom's car broke down again (shocker).
- Caitlyn still hated my guts (And no, I never ratted her out. It was a total coincidence, honestly).

Let's see, what else. Oh yeah, how could I forget?

- The stupid presidential debates.

It was on a Thursday after dinner (tuna casserole, only a notch better than broccoli casserole), that we settled in for the first of three presidential debates. I was thrilled that my hair was coming back in. It was still short but Dad no longer laughed out loud whenever he walked in from work. Mom mentioned how combing your scalp stimulated hair growth so I'd done that until I had dandruff. But that could've been the sunburn.

Dad had been working dawn till dusk with last-minute planning and prep as the countdown was on for the big ground breaking—only twelve days away. Meanwhile Mom was scrambling with the editorials and meetings and other last-ditch efforts to stop him from "desecrating the earth." And so it went...

Once again Tom Brokaw welcomed us, this time to St. Louis where history was being made as the three-way debate between President Bush, Governor Bill Clinton, and Ross Perot was all ready to go. Dad shook his head, still muttering about how Perot had no business on the stage. But there they were, ready to "get it on" like one of the Rocky movies. Only with old guys.

With a yawn, I spread out on the floor, propping my head on my hand as the bickering began. Clinton hammered home his ideals and pleas for change, then Bush, like a grandfather, scowled as though everyone was speaking a language he didn't understand. But Ross Perot, the big-eared Texas billionaire, was sure spicing things up.

Every time I got bored and my eyes went heavy with all the economy talk, Mr. Perot turned the debate into a conversation. To me, he was more like a regular person who'd somehow wandered up on stage and said what he felt. He'd shake his head and gesture from Bush to Clinton, griping about what he called the blame game. He talked about the deficit, dove into the crazy details about how we could fix it. He tossed numbers around and made it sound like all we needed was a new CEO—which I guess the president kind of was. If nothing else, the Perot guy was entertaining, and maybe it was just to spite Mom and Dad, but I found myself cheering him on.

When Clinton spoke in favor of women's rights and lowering the cost of health care, Mom clapped and cheered while Dad folded his arms and groused about paying for such lofty promises. But Clinton made it sound easy. He was calm and smooth, and it was easy to see why he was leading in the polls.

Overall, I couldn't say who won. Mom said Clinton and of course Dad said Bush. At least Perot had an answer of what he would do to solve the problems. But when I said so, Mom and Dad both looked at me like I was a lost puppy.

Being all fired up, it didn't take long for the two of them to get into it, mainly about healthcare. I could see Mom's point that it wasn't right that some people couldn't afford to go to the hospital because they didn't have insurance, or they had crummy insurance that wouldn't pay. Dad said the government wasn't there to hand out insurance to people, which sounded pretty crummy as well.

"What are people supposed to do then?" I asked.

"If people work hard, they don't need a handout," Dad said.

Mom shot a blistering stare his way. "But some people haven't had all the privileges we've enjoyed, Ben."

Dad's face contorted into disbelief. "Oh, please. I work my tail off, every day. Everything we have I've busted my rump to get," he said. Then he noticed Mom's smile. "What?"

"Honey. You do work hard. I know that. Honestly, I do. But think about this, remember when we bought this house, how our parents helped with the down payment? Not everyone has that...opportunity. That's all I'm saying."

Dad's face went red as a brick. He hopped up and started pacing. "So because our parents, not the government, gave us a little help with the house..." he started and then stopped, turning to her. "It's different and you know it."

"Is it?"

Dad spun off, talking loud and furious with flailing arms. "Oh, don't give me that hippie, mumbo-jumbo talk. You sound like a socialist, where everyone should have the same house and the same job and we all hug and sing together. That's not reality, Ana!"

Mom only sat on the couch, smiling, which made Dad pace faster, talk louder, and flail more.

"How could you say that?" he continued, basically arguing with the wall. He turned one way then the other. "I don't receive welfare or take anything from the government. I go to work every single day to put food on the table. And you know how hard I work, even though you're trying to stop the biggest opportunity we've ever had!"

"I'm not trying to ruin your job, honey. We've talked about this."

"Well you keep writing those letters, and then this piece in *Newsweek*, and the interviews. It's embarrassing, Ana."

On television, Tom Brokaw discussed the debate with a republican analyst. Like Mom and Dad, both republicans *and* democrats claimed victory. But Dad no longer seemed interested in politics. And Mom was up on her heels, happy to talk Mega More.

"So, I'm embarrassing you? Is that what this is all about?" she said, her eyes roaring to life, her voice rising to match Dad's intensity.

"Not what I said. But can't you just let it go? It seems everyone in this town is talking about us. The letters to the newspaper, the interviews...that schmuck Mayor Pickens for goodness sakes." He tossed his hands in the air. "I've already been asked if I need to step away from the project."

Dad's admission hit the living room with a thud, leaving everything muted in its aftermath. Only the tired humming of the air conditioner groaned along as Mom parted her lips to speak but then changed her mind.

"Are you serious, Ben?"

Dad drew a long, tired breath. His hair was out of place and dark circles tugged at his eyes. He stopped pacing and stared at the floor. Mom glanced at me, then back to Dad.

"Okay," she said, nodding to herself. "If you want me to drop it, I will." I looked from her to Dad. There was no way he'd let her do that, right?

My dad turned to her, shaking his head. Like he couldn't ask her to stop but he couldn't let her continue. Maybe he knew he'd gone too far because he took a breath and rubbed his hands together. "Let's talk about it, later," he said. "I'm beat."

He kissed her on the cheek and then rubbed the stubble on my head. When he left the room Mom let out a big sigh, staring at a spot on the couch for a minute. I think we all knew we had to stick together, no matter our differences. At least I hoped they did.

I started for the hallway, figuring I'd read Sports Illustrated in bed for a while, when something caught my eye. Mom's book was flipped over on the side table. And right there on the back of the book, staring back at me, was the sun-wrinkled face of Mr. Bardwell.

"He writes books?" I asked, picking up the big block of pages.

"Huh?" Mom said, then noticed the book in my hands. "Oh, Earnest? Yes." Her eyes snapped out of their daze and did that twinkling thing they did when she was happy with me. "You didn't know that?"

I shook my head, leafing through the pages, all crammed with print. Mom patted the seat beside her. "Earnest Bardwell is a well-respected history writer. He lives not too far away, over in Bedford."

I slid onto the couch. "Wait, so he drives over to our house, from Bedford, to fight the Mega More store?" I asked, hardly able to believe that the jokester who'd watched me get my head shaved was some sort of book celebrity. I mean, he wasn't Michael Jordan or anything, but I guess he had fans.

"Here, let me show you," Mom said, suddenly excited at my interest in a book. I handed it to her.

"What's this about?" I asked, seeing the title, *Stripping Appalachia.*

"Well, it's about how the logging industry in the late nineteenth century devastated the forests and mountains and communities of the Appalachian Mountains."

I always had trouble with the centuries. I took a second to do the math. "So, like in the eighteen-hundreds? Who wants to read about that?"

"I do," Mom said, smiling. "Because over a hundred years later, we still haven't learned how to coexist with nature."

That was certainly something my dad would call "new age hippie mumbo jumbo," but I kind of wanted to hear more. "Like the Mega More?"

Mom nodded, sitting up straight. "Exactly, but also things like coal mining and the environment in general."

I was walking a thin line, just on the brink of a sermon. I had to guide her out of the impending lesson. "So what else has old Mr. Bardwell written?"

"Oh gosh. Let's see. He's done several biographies. Fredrick Douglass, Eleanor Roosevelt...he's also done a New Deal series that was adapted into a mini-series on PBS."

"Really? So he *is* kind of famous."

Mom laughed. "Yes, I suppose he is. And he wants to help

me organize a peaceful protest at the Mega More hiring session next week," she said with a quick glance down the hallway.

Oh boy. "What does Dad think?"

Mom tapped my leg as she stood. "What do you *think* he thinks?" I took that to mean that Dad didn't know. She yawned, then leaned over and kissed me on the head. She patted the book. "Go ahead and dive in, if you want. I need to go talk to your father." Another peck on my head. "Goodnight, sweetie."

"Good night," I said, then I called out to her again. "Hey Mom."

She turned around.

"So who won tonight?" I asked and she raised an eyebrow.

"Clinton, of course," she said with a stretch. Then she started down the hallway.

I meant between her and Dad.

I caught up with Dad early the next morning, clanking around in the kitchen. He was pouring coffee into his battered Reynolds Construction mug when he saw me and smiled brightly. "Hey buddy."

"Hey."

He stopped pouring coffee. "You okay?"

"Uh huh. So are you and Mom in a fight?"

He set the mug down and eyed me closely. "We're fine, Marcus, don't worry about us. You know how we get with politics, right?"

I nodded. The counter was covered with sugar and creamer. Mom liked to say that Dad and I had a special gift for making messes. I noticed the newspaper still rolled up on the table. "What if Bill Clinton wins, are you going to be okay then?"

He grimaced, like the coffee was too bitter. "I don't know. Let's try not to think about it, okay?"

"So who do you think won the debate last night?"

Dad shook his head. "Bush mopped the floor with that lib."

I guess both sides could claim victory. "Yeah, but Perot had some good ideas."

Dad cracked up harder than he did watching America's Funniest Home Video's. He rubbed my head and grinned. "About time for another date with the clippers, isn't it?"

"Ha ha."

Unrolling the paper, Dad glanced over the front page with a

large picture of President Bush looking confused as ever under the shining lights of the debate. In the lower corner, there was a small piece about the ground-breaking ceremony.

"Dad?"

"Yeah," he said, looking up.

I didn't know exactly how to say what I wanted to say. Last night it felt like all my thoughts were neatly placed and in order. Now everything was jumbled together. "Do you think that cemetery will be okay, I mean, with all of the traffic and stuff?"

It wasn't exactly what I wanted to ask or how I wanted to ask it, but that was how it came out. Dad sighed, like he knew what I meant. He set the paper to the side. "You know, if it were up to your Mom we'd be living in caves and eating by a campfire every night. Aren't you glad we have electricity and running water? It's called progress."

What I wanted to say, but didn't, was, can't we have progress *and* history?

Speaking of progress, later that morning Cullen and I attacked his lawn with a vengeance. Again, we used my mower and gas, but the way I saw it, Dad would be happy to see us take initiative. Then he could stop moaning about the jungle of a lawn down at the old Ramsey place.

Cullen's yard was full of trash, so we had to clean up before we could mow. We started with the beer cans strewn along the driveway, some hidden in the rolled over grass. Off to the side, caught in the pine trees, were wrappers, plastic grocery bags, and enough cigarette packages to fill two lawn bags. Once we got the old tires out of the way and cleared the obstacles, Cullen cranked up the mower and we started the hack job.

While Cullen mowed, I looked to the windows where the tattered curtains did little to hide the bare walls inside. I thought about the other day, when I'd stuck my head in there. Mom would have said it was none of my business. But the car was in the driveway, and yet no one came out to check on us, or even see who was mowing the grass.

I wandered around, gathering more trash and even finding some newer liquor bottles near the scraggly azaleas beside the front porch. After a while I heard the mower conk out and then the squeaky wobble of the plastic wheels.

"Man, that back hill was a beast," Cullen said, hauling the Murray up to the driveway.

"Is your dad home?" I asked, and he cut his eyes to the house.

"Yeah. He's doing some work in the basement though," he said, tapping the mower with his foot. "Hey, let's get this thing back to your place."

Mom was in the den typing away. I chugged down cold water until my teeth hurt, and I was refilling Cullen's glass when the door swung open and Mom rushed in with some papers. "Hey guys. I'm meeting Earnest at the Mega More hiring session. Can I trust you guys not to shave your heads for the next couple of hours?"

Cullen nearly spilled his water. "The famous author?" he asked, and Mom cut her eyes at me with a smile.

"Yes, the *famous author*," she repeated, setting her reading glasses on the legal pad at the table.

"Can we go?" Cullen asked, smacking his lips. A tingle of panic skittered down my arms. All I could think about were those flat tires on the truck.

Mom shook her head. "No, I don't think it's a good idea. Marcus, your dad would have a fit."

I knew she was thinking about Squabble Creek, and honestly, I was relieved. Besides, I'd rather hop on the skateboard and work on my moves than go hang out with Mom. But it was clear Cullen had other plans. He turned on the charm. "We'll be good, Mrs. Hawthorne. We can even sit in the car. It would be a great educational opportunity."

My mom was no sucker. "Nice try, Cullen, but I think you two should sit this one out. Besides, I don't need any more parents upset with me."

I was about to push her out the door, ready to stay home all by myself again. Especially after we helped Mom load up her poster board signs. One said, *Mega No to Mega More!* Another one read, *Don't sell our history!*

"Man, your mom is awesome!" Cullen held up a sign as though he were practicing. I shot him a pointed look. Now my mom was rad and awesome? Let's not get carried away.

With her signs and notebook in the backseat, Mom hopped into her moody little car. She leaned over to roll down her window. "You guys be good. Honey, if you need anything, call Mrs. Newman next door. Okay?"

I nodded. But no sooner than she got her car aimed in the right direction and began putting down the street, Cullen turned to me with a smile. "Okay, I'll go get my bike and meet you back here. We need to check this out."

"Cullen no, we can't. Seriously," I pleaded.

"Come on, Marcus, let's have a little adventure this summer," he yelled over his shoulder, already halfway down the driveway.

Between my shaved head, my itchy legs, the dunk booth, and the stunt at Squabble Creek, I wasn't sure how much more excitement I could stand. I tried to call out to him but my voice squeaked. Cullen took off down the street. I went inside to change clothes.

We stopped at the Quick Mart where Cullen put air in his leaky tires. With our pockets stuffed full of bubble gum and Lemonheads, we got back on the road, sticking to the sidewalk, Cullen hopping curbs and me hoping not to face plant. As we came to the corner of the Winn Dixie and the Wilson Road Pharmacy, I called for Cullen—who clearly didn't know where he was going but was still in a race to get there. His back tire wobbled as he braked to a skid. He whirled around, and I nearly wrecked to a stop.

"Man, you need new tires," I said between breaths. We faced opposite directions. Both of his tires were slick and cracked on the sides where I could see the threads.

"You stopped me to tell me that?" he said, breathing easy as a nap.

"Oh, no. Um, so after this light is the car wash, and then the Wilson Road Business Center where Mom is, so, let's try to stay out of sight, okay?"

Cullen shrugged. "Okay, I'll follow you."

I nodded, surprised he'd let me take the lead. We coasted past the car wash and I slowed as we came down the hill and down to the parking lot. Weaving around parked cars, we stopped behind a van where we could hide out yet still get a good look at the front of the offices. Cullen pointed to Mom thrusting her sign, reading, *The Dead Abhor the Mega More.*

Wow, I thought, *she sure is pouring it on thick.* And she wasn't alone, there was Mr. Bardwell and a group of Native Americans, some even dressed in full headgear. Everyone thrusting signs in the air.

"This is so awesome," Cullen said, craning his neck around the back of the van. It was a sight. On the other side of the office were two meatheads, sleeves rolled up and guarding the door like Mom and her posse were a serious threat to rush in and take the place down. Meanwhile, several people were coming in or heading out, some shaking their heads and jeering at Mom and Earnest Bardwell.

I'm not sure how long I watched from my spot at the front of the van. But it was kind of wild seeing my mom—maker of dinner, folder of clothes, helper of homework—out there going head-to-head with those people. A few passers-by stopped and asked her questions, and she'd set her sign down and nod and smile, chatting with them or handing out leaflets. Others were not so friendly and would yell nasty things at her, shouting for her and Earnest to go home or get out of town. I felt a surge of fear, and I turned back to see if Cullen was watching, but...

Cullen?

He was already at the curb by the time I could whisper-yell at him. Mom's face froze in shock as she forgot whatever she was chanting, because Cullen had marched over, picked up a sign, and joined in with the chanting and protesting. Mr. Bardwell shot him a smile, and the Native tribe welcomed him in their circle. Mom leaned toward him and he motioned to the van.

I began composing my eulogy.

With a defeated breath, I emerged. Mr. Bardwell smiled. Mom did not. I shuffled forward, in no hurry to get to the curb, hanging my head and preparing for the worst.

I was staring at my feet when a horn blasted me from my thoughts of doom. I shot my head up and came face to grill with a massive truck, eye level with the F-O-R-D on the hood.

"Watch where you're going, punk!" came a voice from beyond the hood. I'd never been called a "punk" before, so I craned my neck and squinted up toward the source. I felt the heat of the engine on my cheeks and sure enough, sticking out from the driver's window, were two bulging eyes underneath the oily brim of a cap. I held up a timid hand and mumbled a quick sorry over the growl of the truck.

He hit the gas the moment my foot hit sidewalk, and the truck lurched forward only to stop again. The two meatheads stared at me like I'd crawled out of a dumpster. I looked over at Mom.

"I told you not to come here, Marcus," she said, her sign forgotten.

I was beyond embarrassed. First, I nearly got creamed by the truck, and now everyone waiting to get in and apply for jobs stood gawking at us. Cars lined up behind the truck guy, still growling with that pulsing red glare he'd now fixed on Mom. Then with a squeal of tires, he bolted up the parking lot.

"Wow, that dude needs a hug," Cullen said.

The only thing helping me keep it together were the two police cruisers parked under a cherry tree near the median of the lot. The officers watched intently as the truck tore into a parking spot, nearly ramming the parked cars as he squeezed into a space. I swallowed hard as the short man hopped out of his big truck and strutted down toward the offices. Mom was still waiting for an explanation.

"I know, we were only going to watch, but..." I gestured to Cullen, who was chanting "No More Mega More!" at the top of his lungs.

"You shouldn't be here," she said, but the fire in her eyes said something else.

This whole time I'd been trying to decide what side I was on, and although I could see what Dad was saying—about progress and development—I knew there was a place for history, too. My body still tingled from my brush with death, and maybe my brain had been rattled out of whack. It's hard to say. It could have been Mom's passion or Cullen's unconquered energy. Maybe it was even Mr. Bardwell's quiet confidence. But for the first time in my life, I made my own decision.

"I'm staying."

With that, I strode over to the protest section. My hands trembled as I picked up the only sign left. *Keep Squabble Creek Beautiful!*

Mom looked at the sign and then at me. Then she smiled. "Okay then."

The day was beautiful as I joined the march, only a few dots of clouds and a slight breeze that was picking up a little as the police stood to the side, directing traffic and keeping order. It didn't even feel like me, what I was doing. But it did feel right, and that was what mattered.

I picked up the pace, feeling good about being on the right side. And then the angry man from the truck stomped up to the curb.

He slunk past us, muttering something about stupid kids and spitting on the sidewalk as he took his place in the Mega More employment line. Like anyone would want to hire that guy. Thankfully, just behind him, the two policemen strolled down to patrol things a little more carefully.

The officers said we were free to march as long as we weren't impeding traffic. With that said, Cullen and I took to the median near the street and had a blast. A few people honked as they passed. I was starting to get into this whole protest thing. Cullen made up this little dance he did with his sign, one similar to my living room dance. Soon I was dancing too.

I was laughing so hard I didn't even see the *WRGT News* truck pull into the lot and set up for broadcast.

My sign fell to the curb as Martha Flintlock hustled to the scene, her massive bangs bouncing as she shouldered her way into the fray, thrusting her microphone under the chin of anyone willing to talk. It didn't take long for things to get crazy, making the news in Newburg was a pretty big deal. In fact, the last time I could remember *WRGT* in town it was to interview Gordy Simpson, who'd recently cracked the record books for his massive collection of Garbage Pail Kids.

Now here she was again, stirring things up, as the wide-eyed crazies poured out of the stores and jostled for position.

"Dude, let's get down there!" Cullen said, grabbing my arm. We sifted through the bodies and around the news truck at the curb where Martha was interviewing Mr. Bardwell. Several of the Mega More hopefuls gunned for the camera, waving and trying to get a few seconds of airtime while Earnest struggled to be heard over the crowd noise. Martha nodded and smiled, revealing her ultra-white camera-ready smile.

The crowd pushed and Mom squeezed my hand. The meatheads shut the doors to the office as the line of people fought for the camera, waving at Martha like she was a game show host. *Pick me! Pick me!*

My throat tightened as more people pushed toward the sidewalk. Mom stood with Mr. Bardwell as he tried to relay the importance of Newburg's responsibility to Squabble Creek and its natural beauty and historical significance. But I don't think

Martha was there for history or Mr. Bardwell—she was out for blood.

She blew at her bangs while he spoke, her eyes cutting back and forth from him to the crowd with furious nods. Then, before he'd even finished, she thanked him and moved the microphone to her next target: Mom.

Martha was firing away with her next question when the shouting behind us grew angrier. In the distance, past the parking lot and the traffic of Wilson Road, a wall of dark storm clouds rolled over the horizon, about to clash with the sunny day. Martha struggled to hold the microphone steady in the swell of the crowd. "Mrs. Hawthorne, with Mr. Bardwell here you've been perhaps Mega More's biggest opponent, but isn't it true your very own husband works for Reynolds Construction, who will be among the contractors to help build the store?"

I nearly fell into the bodies closing in on us. With all that had happened I hadn't had time to worry about Dad. And now, here was the camera, trained on my face like a rocket launcher. If Dad saw me there, *when* he saw me there, at the protest with Mom on the news, well, I couldn't imagine. But those worries had little time to fester, because the red-faced man who'd almost nailed me with his truck was coming at us, pointing and yelling and even more red-faced than before.

I started to back away. Everything was spinning out of control. Trouble was in the air, hanging over us like the dark approaching clouds. It was like the air had infected the sneering faces surrounding us and it was spreading like a virus.

"Get out of here, all of you," the man shouted at us.

I turned to bolt but ran smack into Cullen, who was staring right into the man's scraggly face without a trace of fear in his eyes. "Shut up, you stupid hick!"

Okay, we were officially dead. Martha motioned toward the confrontation and the cameraman swiveled to the action. The glare of the lights burned hot on my forehead. Truck-man took a step forward, but the crowd was too thick for him to get through. Martha's smile doubled at this new development unfolding while the cameras were rolling.

Unbelievably, my mom was still trying to answer Martha's question. But she'd been drowned out by the chorus of agitated job seekers. "Go home!" someone jeered. It was clear we were severely outnumbered. It felt like the crowd was about to swallow us whole.

Then came the chanting. "We Want Mega More!"

We stumbled one way, then the other way. Truck-man shook his fists, his stinky breath hot on my back when Cullen spun around, cupping his hands around his mouth and yelled, "You go home!"

But that only got everyone more fired up, and soon the chanting became screaming, then stomping, and I waited for the place to erupt. Last spring, I'd watched on the news as the LA riots had raged, with the fires and the destruction, and when someone took Mr. Bardwell's sign I thought that's where we were headed.

Mom swooped in and grabbed our wrists, yanking Cullen and me away from the mess as Martha and the camera backed away to fully capture the confrontation.

By then I was nearly in shock, too paralyzed with fear to do much on my own. Our little group retreated to the other end of the offices, but that didn't work either, because the office managers waved us off and asked us to leave the building. Martha and her cameraman spanned the chaos, then rushed back into the meat of things to interview the throng of Mega More supporters.

I looked to Cullen, glaring and grinning at Truck-man, who was adjusting his belt like he wanted to hand out a spanking.

When he finally headed for the office doors, Cullen turned to me with a grin. "Yeah, he'll make a great stock boy."

Mom pulled us together. "Is everyone okay?"

I nodded. Mr. Bardwell nodded. "Makya? How about you guys, you okay?"

"Yes, we're fine." The Monacan Tribe stood stock still and proud as the mob of people applying for jobs yelled and called us names that would have gotten me grounded for a month.

"Well, I think I'm done for today," Mom said, and then set her eyes on me. "Marcus, this is why I didn't want you here. You never know what's going to happen."

I nodded, still shaken from the mob. But my worry was now two-fold. What exactly would happen to me when Dad saw the news tonight?

For Cullen it was all a day at the beach. In fact, he was still holding up his sign defiantly, thrusting it like a sword into the darkening sky. His eyes were full of fight, and I was starting to think he liked the agitating and protesting more than the actual cause. The two police officers worked to break up the crowd, which settled considerably after the camera lights went dark. Martha was back in the van, pursing her lips and staring into her compact just as the rain started.

When a few more policemen arrived, they strolled toward us. I think Dad said that we had twelve police officers, so it was quite the show of force for them to be out in such numbers at the business center. One was old and kind of plump and the other was tall and skinny and looked barely out of high school. He was the one who tipped his hat to us.

"You guys okay?"

Mom nodded. "Oh yes, we're fine."

"Okay, I think you guys should pack it up for today. We don't want to have a situation."

"The situation is at Squabble Creek," Cullen said without

the slightest hint of hesitation in his voice. I'd always been taught to call police officers "sir." Cullen called them cops.

The heavier officer turned to him, took in his skater clothes and bad haircut. "Well, that's not our business. This is our business, making sure there's no trouble."

"They're the trouble; we're only trying to be heard," Cullen replied.

"Well, I'd say you've done that. Now let's go."

It was dark as night in my room. A steady rain fell against my window. I glanced at the clock—6:09—the local news was broadcasting the big story. Martha Flintlock was no doubt recounting the unruly scene at the Business Center today. I'd told Cullen I wasn't feeling well when we'd gotten back home, which was true. I felt horrible.

Dad had pulled in a little bit ago, and now, as the thunder rumbled, I took inventory in my room. Two cloudy glasses of water and a half-eaten bag of Mom's trail mix. I figured I could hole up in here for the next week without coming out. But I never got the chance.

Mom peeked in to tell me it was time for dinner. She shot me a wink that I took to mean that I might not be facing the guillotine.

Baked chicken and brown rice. Oh joy. I took my place and prepared for the worst, but miraculously the television was off. The story had probably already run on *WRGT*—they would have led with it for sure. Maybe this would buy me some time. I'd only have to pray that the newspaper wouldn't run the story of the mom and son protest team at the Wilson Road Business Center.

"Hey kiddo," Dad said, taking his seat. "I figured you were down at Cullen's."

His tone gave nothing away. I managed to mumble something about not feeling well, resting in my room. Mom set the chicken on the table and cut her eyes to me. If I didn't know better, I would have thought she looked a little shaky herself.

"So," Dad said. "What's new? Do anything fun today?"

Mom and I locked eyes. My heart did a little rain dance in my chest as my stomach flopped over on its back to play dead. Dad forked a chicken breast from the pan and plopped it down on his plate. He smiled real big. "Well?"

He glanced from me to Mom, Mom to me. Game over. Right then and there I knew that he knew his one and only son had stabbed him square between the shoulder blades. After all he'd done for me, providing this warm but gross meal of rice with his muscle and sweat. And here I'd left him hanging when it counted the most.

All I could do was stammer through a response. "I uh, we..."

Dad nodded, whipping out the linen napkin Mom insisted on us using to save a few trees. Dad liked to joke that soon we'd be using corn cobs in the bathroom, but so far we'd stuck to good old Charmin. Smoothing the napkin over his lap, he set his eyes on me with a finger to his chin.

"Did you go to the park? Maybe build a model airplane?"

My tongue tried to retreat down my throat. Dad shook his head. "Nope, that's not it either. Oh, wait. I know!" he said, snapping his fingers. "How about a run-in with local law enforcement, that's it, isn't it?"

Oh boy. I stared at my empty plate, avoiding his knowing gaze. Where it was usually Mom with the upper hand, Dad was no slouch. And he was almost enjoying himself. I peeked up to find him scooping rice onto his plate without a complaint, only casting a sharp gaze Mom's way. I braced myself for the impending fight. Not a fun fight either, a bad one—the only ones they seemed to have anymore.

Dad set his plate down, about to kick things off. But before he could blame Mom, before she took the fall for me, I came clean. "It wasn't Mom's fault. Cullen and I rode our bikes down to see what was going on. She didn't even know!"

He took a breath so big it seemed to pull every molecule of oxygen from the room. "Oh really, that Cullen kid had something to do with this? Well, what do you know? Never would have guessed it."

Mom piped in, "Ben, don't blame Marcus. Or Cullen. Besides, it wasn't all that bad. Sure, there were a few angry folks out there, but nothing we couldn't handle."

"Couldn't handle?" Dad shook his head. The room fell quiet. No one had touched their food when Dad, his voice a little wrenched, told us how he'd heard from the crew we'd been at the business center. He'd heard about the mob and the cops and even the news team.

Mom smiled. She dished up some chicken and set it on my plate, explaining to Dad how it wasn't so bad—which was news to me—and he even smirked when she said how we were within our rights until the news arrived and from there everything got so crazy.

Dad looked at Mom, then to me. And then he almost smiled as he turned toward the living room. "Hey, why aren't we watching it, anyway?"

Mom laughed nervously. "Oh, um..."

Dad hopped up, and in a few quick strides he was in the living room turning on the television. The next thing I knew, we were all in the room watching the evening news. But it was only weather.

"Looks like we missed it," he said.

Mom smiled. "Oh, I'm recording it."

"Mom!"

She smiled. "What? For Cullen."

With that, she pressed a button and rewound the tape. An Olympic commercial flashed across the screen. I'd almost forgotten about the Dream Team, back in the simple days of my youth before my clashes with police.

Dad grabbed the remote and Mom rolled her eyes. He pressed play as the big blocky letters from Roanoke's WRGT News team hit the screen and a smiling anchorman straightened some papers and smiled.

"Good evening. We had quite the scene over at the Wilson Road Business Center in Newburg earlier today, where a small group of protesters clashed with applicants for the new Mega More store coming to town. Martha Flintlock reporting..."

The camera panned the business center, and suddenly there I was, my face a pale sheet of terror as I stood somewhere behind Mom and Cullen.

"I'm here with Ana Hawthorne, a Newburg citizen protesting the construction of the new Mega More Super Store. Ana, tell us why you're here today."

"Well, Martha," Mom began, her voice calm and sharp. "Again, we're here not so much against Mega More, but the proposed site of the new store. Squabble Creek is home to one of the state's oldest cemeteries and we just think that there are other, more reasonable sites—"

"Yes, but City Council has already appropriated the Squabble Creek site and the decision has been made. So what is the goal of this little protest?"

Dad chuckled as Mom's face made it clear she didn't like being interrupted or the use of the word "little." I'd been too tangled up in fear to catch it.

Mom flashed Martha a fake smile then continued where she left off. "Like the Wilson Road area, which is already zoned commercial and makes far more sense..."

That's when Martha asked the question about Dad and right about the time everything went nuts. Cullen yelled back, and Dad rolled his eyes but then he muttered something under his breath and rewound the tape a bit.

"What is it?" Mom asked.

"Him," Dad said, pausing the tape, freezing the screen on Truck-man. A few squiggly lines passing over his shirt.

"Kirk. Kirk, uh...what is it?" He slapped at his leg with the remote. "Kirk Pike," he said louder. "He took a job with us as a few months back. Worked a week and then quit coming around. Laziest piece of..." Mom coughed, raising her brow. Dad blinked and changed gears. "Good for nothing, that's all."

"That guy?" I pointed to the truck guy. "He yelled at us all day long," I said, sensing a change in the tide. I glared at the man's bright red face on television. The veins bulging through the hair on his neck. "And at Mom," I added quickly.

Dad stared at the screen like he wanted to bust through it. Then he looked at his feet, breathing hard through his nose like he did when he got fired up about something.

Mom put her arm around his waist. "You okay, hon?"

"I'm fine," Dad said, as Mom snuggled her cheek into his chest. Dad shook his head, his expression blank. "I should have driven over. The guys said it was just some arguing."

"It was." Mom looked up to Dad with a smile. "It was nothing."

Personally, I thought it was a lot more than nothing. Dad shook his head some more. Mom hugged him tighter. "Ben, we were fine."

Dad pointed the remote and pressed play again, and we watched our day unfold from a different angle. And I have to say, it wasn't my greatest angle.

"Look at Marcus," Dad said, gesturing to the shaky footage capturing my doe-eyed horror. I was crouched low somewhere behind my sign in the background, but that was mainly because

I'd realized we were going to be on the news and Dad would see us.

The camera found its way back to Martha, who could hardly contain her glee. "As you can see, tempers are flaring."

Martha played up the scene, as though it were more than a few county folks shouting at us, which seeing it now on television didn't look like much at all. Mom was right. It wasn't all that newsworthy, except in Newburg, I guess.

Dad grinned, even chuckling a little as we retreated. Martha interviewed some of the potential employees, one of whom said that we were dumber than a bucket of worms. Whatever that meant.

The television cut back to the newsroom, where the anchors smiled and said things like, "Quite the scene there today," and "Well that was interesting."

We were all giggling by the time Dad declared he'd had enough and turned it off. Mom seemed as surprised as me about Dad's reaction to the whole thing. And even more surprised when he sat back down to the table, took a big old bite of chicken and looked us over. "My two little hippies."

There was no arguing as we got back to dinner. For the first time in a while, we talked about school shopping, maybe catching a movie over the weekend. Family stuff. Politics and Mega More, at least for a night, were cast aside without another thought. After dinner we stepped outside, where the clouds had broken apart and the sun was making one last go at it.

Mom weeded her garden while Dad and I tossed the football around and, without saying a word about it, it was like we all had decided to appreciate each other a little more that night.

For the past two summers we'd gone camping with the Peebles up at the Blue Ridge Parkway. We'd load up around mid-July and take off for a week in the woods—or until we were all ready for a shower. But it seemed nothing this summer ran on schedule.

I was with Dad in the basement on Thursday evening. The plan was for me to go camping with the Peebles so Dad could attend the ceremony, and Mom could do whatever she was plotting, and maybe they could finally put this thing to rest. Dad had come home on time for once and we were trying to find the tent and the gear among the clutter on the shelves when Mom started stomping and squealing upstairs.

"It's here! It's here!"

We rushed up to the living room and found her cutting the tape on a box with a kitchen knife. "*Newsweek!*" she gasped. Dad arched his eyebrows.

"The big time."

Mom flung open the flaps on the box and then pulled out a shiny, crisp edition of *Newsweek*. Governor Clinton was on the cover, mobbed by a crowd of supporters like a movie star. His face was chiseled in thought as a teary-eyed girl reached out to him. I peeked back at Dad, but instead of rolling his eyes or making a snide comment, he knelt beside her and set a hand on Mom's shoulder. She rested her hand on his and closed her eyes. Then, after a sniffle, she flipped open the magazine.

"Okay, let's hear it," Dad said, moving to the couch. I plunked down beside him and we sat waiting as Mom smiled, found her piece, then turned and held it up for us to see. A one-page story with a picture of the planet at the top.

"'Developing Mother Nature', by Ana Hawthorne."

She cleared her throat dramatically, her eyes sparkling with her smile as she began. Dad and I listened carefully, and to my amazement Dad didn't snicker or sigh, or groan even one single time. A few times I glanced over to him, and I couldn't quite put my finger on what I saw: pride? Love? Interest? Whatever it was he just sat there with me, hanging on every word.

Something had changed with Dad after the newscast the other night. He was a little quieter, thinking more, joking less. And I think Mom had noticed it too. Dinners were tame, both the food and the discussion. Even when Mom tossed out a few barbs, trying to get something out of him about the big groundbreaking on Saturday, it didn't shake him up in the slightest.

When Mom finished her story I clapped and whistled. Her eyes beamed and she mentioned that the editors might be interested in future pieces. I was sure once the issue hit the stands Mom would be taking interviews and maybe even some questions from Mr. Carraway. I doubted she'd give Martha Flintlock the time of day.

So with all that happening, I couldn't think about camping. I told my parents I was staying.

"Are you sure?" Mom said, still holding the magazine.

Dad frowned at me. "Well, things are going to be hectic around here, Marcus. With the big ceremony, I've got a lot of prep to do."

"Me too," Mom said with a devilish smirk.

Yet even that didn't wipe the smile off my dad's face. "Oh boy."

"I still have a few tricks up my sleeve," Mom said. But they weren't fighting anymore, it was getting stranger by the second. All the more reason not to leave.

Dad got to his feet and set his arms around Mom. "Marcus, you really want to stay?"

"Oh yeah," I nodded. "I don't want to miss this."

Not only that, I was still bound and determined to get that kick-flip done before summer. That and biking with Cullen, along with whatever was about to go down with Mom and Dad, sounded way better than sharing mosquito bites and beans while talking Mega More with the Peebles. And just thinking of the Peebles, the phone rang in the kitchen.

I hopped up and snatched the phone. Danny was already talking before I could finish saying hello.

"Dude. I saw you on the news the other day. What in the world?"

"Oh, well, we were—"

"So what time will you get there tomorrow? I've got tons of marshmallows, but you may want to be sure and bring some extra Hershey bars because I already caught Mikey gnawing on one of them. Oh, and did you get your fishing license? I got mine yesterday."

The old me would have caved. I would have laughed and let Danny ramble on and soon I'd be in the truck with Dad headed up the mountain. But I wasn't the old me anymore, and as I listened to the chaos in the background—the constant noise that seemed to follow the Peebles wherever they went—I pictured Coach Peebles fussing about, searching the campground for his boots while Danny's mom griped about bug spray. I was already done with it.

I wasn't in the mood to hang out with the Peebles, answering questions about Mom, or Cullen, or my clothes and music. Danny was still going on about S'mores as I peeked into the living room where Mom and Dad were still locked tight in an embrace, looking at the pile of glossy magazines on the floor.

I laughed, thinking, yeah, someone had to keep an eye on these two. "Hey Danny? Actually, I don't think I'm going to make it," I said with a wince.

"Huh? Wait, don't tell me you all aren't coming until Saturday?"

"No, uh, Dad's got the ground-breaking Saturday. And Mom's got an interview, so—"

"An interview? For trying to stop Newburg from actually becoming, like, a real town? Man, Marcus, what's going on with you? Everyone saw you and that Cullen kid on TV. You do know that you're gonna be the laughingstock of the school this year, right?"

I rubbed my head, urging the stubble to grow out. "Gee, thanks."

"Look man, I gotta run. Oh. the baseball team made the finals, we're going to Richmond next week, not that you care. Have fun with your new delinquent friend."

A click and the phone went dead. Mom and Dad had already retreated into the den. I stood in the kitchen, staring at the barnyard wallpaper, wondering how things got so complicated.

FRIDAY MORNING. The day before ground-breaking and things were no closer to getting normal in our house. Mom worked the phone, pacing like crazy and using her adult voice.

Dad had three dress shirts and both his ties laid out on the couch as he tried to decide what to wear. Mom covered the phone with one hand, helping him choose, even as she spoke openly about her plans to thwart the whole venture.

Since the other day it had been this way. No arguing, only constant touching. Hugs and kisses. Dad said Mom should do what she felt she had to do. Mom said Dad should go with the blue shirt because it brought out his eyes. I mean, what in the world?

When it got to be too much I set out for Cullen's house. On my board, I kicked the tail but the wheels refused to leave the ground. I pushed off and coasted down the street.

I still felt bad about the way things went with Danny, but the morning sun buzzed bright and golden, erasing my doubts. I figured Cullen would have some adventure already mapped out for us by the time I got to his house.

The big Buick was tilted up on a jack, a blue tarp draped over the hood, anchored by large rocks and logs. I didn't think the neighbors cared too much for Cullen's moving in, or what Dad called the wondrous things they'd done for the neighborhood.

I took a breath and pulled back the creaky screen door. I knocked, then waited. And waited. I knocked again and waited some more, leaning left and peeking through the streaky front window through to the back window where a dusty curtain filtered the rays of sun piercing the dingy house. I placed my hands up to block the sun and get a better view.

"You spying on me?"

I jumped, nearly falling over the railing. I spun around to find Cullen on his bike, his dark brown eyes sizing me up.

"What? Uh, no, I was just seeing if you wanted to hang out," I said. "I mean, we're not camping this weekend now," I continued, talking fast like I do when I'm nervous. "See, my mom's piece in *Newsweek* came out, so she's really excited and…"

"Hang on, hang on," he said holding a hand up to derail my freight train of sentences. Cullen was thirteen and I still had a month to go, but he seemed a whole lot older than me. He set his bike against the car and then leaned back on his elbows. "So what did your dad think of our protest?"

"That's the thing." I shrugged, hopping down the steps and over to the Buick. Tree sap and grit dotted the windshield. Clumps of leaves clogged the hood and buried the wipers. "He's fine with it."

"Seriously? That's cool."

I told him about the other night, with the news, and Kirk Pike, and all about *Newsweek*. I mentioned the ground-breaking ceremony. How it was the Twilight Zone at my house.

When I said that Cullen sprang to life, jumping up and clasping his hands. "Oh snap! The ground-breaking ceremony!"

"Yeah, I know. It's tomorrow."

"No. Look!" Cullen grabbed my shoulders, his eyes wide and his smile big as he turned me around to face my house. The orange Beetle sat at the curb. The car full of college girls pulling in behind it. Mr. Bardwell and my father shook hands, nodding and smiling like they weren't sworn enemies, before my dad laughed, hopped in his truck, and backed out of the driveway.

Cullen slapped my back. "Well this is it, Marcus, the eleventh hour. And it looks like our only hope is one last strategic planning committee meeting!"

The Mega More ground-breaking was the biggest event in Newburg since the Maple Run Cineplex arrived a few years back. Squabble Creek was all decked out for the occasion. The area near the stage was trimmed and groomed, the entrance was lined with orange cones and flags. *Event Parking* signs flickered in the abundant morning sun. Cars lined the dirt road, the wildflowers and brush flattened by trucks and machines and flatbed trailers.

Everyone was ready to go to work. Including us.

Cullen and I took it all in from our post behind the chestnut tree. We traded off the binoculars, surveying the crowd and waiting for the signal. I spotted Dad, looking as uncomfortable as ever in his starched blue shirt as he sat with all the suits in attendance.

The ceremony itself was closed to the public. Only local and state politicians along with a few select businessmen and bankers had been invited. Dad, being on the construction team, had scored third row seats.

We snuck between cars, down to the bulldozers where we took cover. From there we had a better angle on the newly erected platform. Cullen was giddy as ever, but I wasn't sure how this was all going to play out. My biggest fear was that Dad was going to denounce me as his son when it was all over. Then again, the way he was acting lately, shaking hands with Bardwell and all, maybe not. Either way, I'd chosen my side at the business center, and now it was time to fight for what was right.

Neat rows of chairs faced the stage, and farther back, us. My gaze wandered over the machinery to the flattened grass and crushed wildflowers. I thought about my quiet visit down here with Mom, the rebuttal visit with Dad, then of course the dangerous tire-flattening prank with Cullen.

Cullen nudged me as Dad's boss, Mitch Reynolds, arrived in a black SUV. He came out smiling, nodding, and fiddling with his jacket. He shook Dad's hand formally before he took his seat. Mitch was a few years younger than Dad but was already bald. I'd heard Mom say how he was a rich daddy's boy who was biding his time until he could take over the company. Secretly, I think Dad agreed with her.

Now, only thirty yards away, it was easy to see that Dad would rather be working. While he loved the building part of his job, he hated all the schmoozing and bureaucracy. Now he was swimming in it.

I watched him flop his hands down in his lap, then to his sides. I was glad he wasn't taking the podium today. Not after his showing at the council meeting. Sure enough, he was stiff and rigid, his size thirteen's tapping away at the freshly trimmed grass. Cullen nudged me, and I passed the binoculars.

The weather was cooperating as it was only in the high seventies. There were maybe fifty or so people there, mostly in suits, chatting and laughing loudly under the stream of morning sun amid the normally quiet countryside.

It was strange to see all the colorful Mega More banners and streamers strewn up and swaying in the breeze. With such a festive atmosphere, it was hard not to get caught up in the hoopla—the fancy white tent over the platform, the suits onstage, their backs to us, turning and laughing, pointing and gesturing, taking in the great view of the creek with the hillside in the background.

It made me furious. Couldn't they see what was at stake? If it was worth pointing and ogling, wasn't it worth saving?

Cullen snickered as Mayor Pickens hobbled up to the podium to kick things off. He welcomed everyone on behalf of the city council to the long-awaited "Big Dig." He lowered the microphone. In front of the stage sat five sparkling new shovels, hard hats resting on the handles, reserved for the row of men who looked like they wouldn't know which end to pick up.

"Thanks to our community of developers, we are experiencing the growth and expansion of progress..."

Our mayor went down the usual list of great things the Mega More would do for Newburg: jobs, economy, oh and the property taxes. My heart kicked into gear. It was just about go-time.

Even from our place behind the machinery, it was clear the mayor was enjoying his moment in the sun. With all those big-time donors in one place, he could hardly contain himself. I spied one last look at my father. I hoped he knew that I was only doing what I thought was right.

"Now, you've heard enough from this old blowhard. Please give a warm welcome to our very own state senator, Mr. Chandler Hoard."

After a round of polite applause, State Senator Hoard shook hands with Mayor Pickens, who held onto his shoulder like it was a life raft in stormy seas.

Breaking away from the mayor's clutches, Senator Hoard took the podium. He adjusted his jacket and raised the microphone. He took a breath and worked the audience. But before he could speak came a blur of gray flapping across the field behind him.

My breath caught and Cullen whispered something I can't

repeat. I shifted, straining to follow as the majestic heron stretched out and glided toward the stage.

A few *oohs* and *ahhs* fell over the audience as the heron then swung up to the air, his impressive wingspan catching the wind beneath him as he swooped down and settled himself on a freshly cut stump just in front of the big, bright Mega More truck.

Senator Chandler pretended nothing happened. "Thank you all, really. I'm so happy to be back in Newburg today…"

As the senator spoke, the heron seemed to be watching, perched on stilts, his regal profile serving as a reminder of what was about to be destroyed. It was something I knew I'd never forget.

Right then, two cars rambled down Squabble Creek Road and my throat nearly closed altogether. I knew it was coming, but that didn't make it any easier. The cars slowed to a crawl as they came around the bend, and Cullen turned to me with a nod. I nodded back as my mouth went dry.

The senator carried on. "In these economic times, it's the prosperity of this small town that puts my heart at ease, to know that nearly one-thousand jobs will be available when you figure in construction, laborers, planners…"

His words boomed over the cemetery. Cullen nodded. It was time. I took a deep breath to calm my nerves. This was actually happening. The old Beetle chugged down the drive, an orange glow in a cloud of dust. A few murmurs came from the seats as the Beetle warbled to a halt. Behind it was another car. Then a van showed up.

And still the stoic heron looked on.

Mr. Bardwell emerged from the car. Cullen popped out from our hiding spot behind the tree, now in plain view of the ceremony. Dad didn't seem to notice, staring blankly as the senator yapped on in the name of prosperity.

A few crows cawed from the trees. The senator paused and turned slightly and saw the heron, then us. With great effort I took a step out from the dozer, into open field and plain view, just as the senator got back to his audience and pressed on.

"With the expansion of Squabble Creek Road, I think this town will receive the boost it needs, and I envision more stores and more expansion..."

Mr. Bardwell led the way, marching ahead with his sign high in the air. The girls followed, even Ethan was there, along with the Monacan tribe. Mom's whole army had come for one last fight. She handed Cullen and me our signs and set her arm around my shoulders. Together, we started forward. We'd circled the wagons and now we headed straight for the mayor.

A murmur came over the crowd. Senator Hoard paused again before he awkwardly turned to glance over his shoulder at the platoon marching across the field. This time he wasn't smiling. No one smiled upon seeing us. Dad's jaw tightened as the senator cleared his throat, gripped the podium, and stumbled over more figures and statistics in a hurry. Like he was trying to wrap things up.

"I hope to be back here again for the opening of the Mega More. Thank you."

After another round of applause. Mayor Pickens wobbled up to the podium, frazzled as ever as he gave a stammering welcome to a Mr. Greg Hatters of LLI Investments Group.

We stopped at the caution tape behind the stage. Only a thin stream of yellow dividing us from them.

Mr. Hatters charged up to the podium, tossing a quick glance over his shoulder as he thanked the mayor (who by now looked like he'd been back in the dunk tank), and nodded to the senator. I guess it was his turn to talk about progress.

"This is only Phase One of our vision for Squabble Creek. I

see restaurants and hotels, a hub of commerce and prosperity that will take Newburg to where it needs to go..."

I took a step forward, right against the tape. "And where does it need to go?"

Some rumbling in the seats and suddenly all eyes were on me. I forced my feet to be steady, holding a sign that read, *This Land Is My Land, Too.*

Mr. Hatters turned awkwardly and cut a razor thin smile my way. "Uh, what's that, kid?"

"Where is that heron supposed to go?" I pointed over to the heron. I couldn't believe what I was doing or saying, but before I could think much about it, the heron came to my rescue, choosing that moment to spring from the stump and spread its wings. With three gaping flaps he landed on Dad's ripper—the bulldozer with a claw-like attachment.

Mr. Hatter turned to the mayor with a glare that could sear steel. "I uh," he half turned, still smiling for the crowd. "Well son, there are plenty of trees here, I think we can all get along?"

I was stunned by the heron's heroic role in our efforts. Cullen edged up beside me. "Yeah, how about we come and pave over your lawn. Maybe rip up the woods around your hunting cabin?" he said, his voice loud and confident.

Mr. Bardwell stepped up beside him. Mom stood proudly beside me. Mr. Reynolds turned to my dad as Mr. Pickens rocketed from his chair like he was Carl Lewis.

"Kid, this isn't a meeting, it's a ceremony," the mayor shouted, looking to the caution tape for security. Then he addressed Mom. "Ah, Mrs. Hawthorne, I should've known. Please, feel free to lodge your complaints at the next city council meeting, but for now please, go back to—oh, no. No, no, no..."

The mayor's wobbly gaze shot past us. His shoulders slumped and he let out a long groan that was picked up by the mic. All heads turned at the sound of gravel crunching, as the

WRGT van came bouncing down the path, leaving a new cloud of dust in its wake.

Our beloved mayor—a guy who usually loved nothing more than a rolling camera— wrenched the microphone from its holder with a screech and nearly knocked Mr. Hatter off the platform. "Look, this is not the time or place for protests!" he said, his voice cracking and shrill.

"According to the first amendment it is," said Mr. Bardwell. In his t-shirt and khakis, he looked ready for a fight as he stepped closer to the tent. His powerful voice needed no amplifier as he called out. "We have every right to be here."

Mitch Reynolds stood and pointed in our direction while barking into my dad's ear. But Dad only stared out straight ahead to Mom and me. And maybe it was the morning sun casting shadows, but I thought I saw the makings of a smile on his face.

Whatever few seconds of calm the heron provided vanished in an instant, as three squad cars—comprising nearly half of Newburg's fleet—came careening down the gravel road. Martha Flintlock wasted no time leading her cameraman into the mix, where Dad was still in his seat, Mom was hoisting her sign, and the mayor was spouting off to whoever would listen. Standing up to an army of suits, my feet turned to ice blocks. For me it was the business center all over again.

"This is the last time I'm going to ask you to leave!" Mayor Pickens shrieked, pointing to the approaching squad cars and completely abandoning his campaign voice. Senator Chandler Hoard leaned over to one of the other suits, wiggling in his seat and searching for a way out of this mess. For him this was probably nothing more than a quick and easy photo op, but now things were getting ugly as Mr. Bardwell, Cullen, the four college girls, and the Monacans stood, arms clasped and, peacefully behind the tent, forming a human chain.

Mom took my arm in hers and we joined the links. To the camera, we must have looked ridiculous. A rag-tag bunch who stood no chance against the Goliath store that was about to rip into the land and pile up the tax dollars while flooding little Newburg with low prices. But not to me. To me, I was part of something big.

Mitch Reynolds, probably wondering how he'd explain this to his father, shook his head and cursed at us. Then he turned his glare to my dad, yelling loud enough for everyone to hear.

"Isn't that your wife? And your kid? You said you would talk to her." His face glowered, and even from where I stood I could see the vein pulsing on his forehead. And his voice cracked worse than mine. "This is no good, Ben. No good at all."

I only watched Dad, still ignoring his boss. I'm not sure if he even heard him. He seemed to be mulling something over in his head as Mayor Pickens tromped toward the police officers, screaming orders and motioning back at the hippie brigade ruining his big moment.

"Can't you control that woman?" Mitch Reynolds shouted at Dad, the only one still sitting in his chair. The guy was bent over, hovering over my dad, pointing toward the protesters. "You need to do something!"

As though he'd come to a decision, my dad finally turned to Mitch Reynolds. With a nod he got to his feet. He towered over his boss as he set one hand on his shoulder, and I read his lips as he uttered two simple words. "I quit."

He started our way, all the stress and worry over the past few months drifting off his shoulders like morning mist. Mitch Reynolds called out to him, eyes wide in disbelief.

"Ben. Hey Ben, think about what you're doing."

Dad walked. He walked away from the biggest job Newberg had ever seen. He walked away from the mayor, flitting around, becoming more maniacal by the second. He walked from the tent, where our mortified state senator was out of his chair, scurrying down the rickety stairs of the stage, his hands out as he barked "no comment" into Martha Flintlock's microphone. He walked from the mad scramble, where seats fell and banners were trampled, as suits and councilmen blamed each other for why the ceremony went up in smoke.

My dad walked toward us. And his face was as calm as the heron on the ripper. He stepped over the spilled chairs as he plodded through the chaos and the golden shovels. He stopped at the tape line and regarded our little human chain, then glanced back to his boss, who was still whining. "You can't be serious, Ben. What are you going to do, stop Mega More?"

Dad shrugged. And when he smiled at me, I thought yeah, maybe we *could* stop Mega More. This guy had taken on a train, of course he could take on the store. And with that, he ducked under the tape and officially crossed enemy lines.

My mom let her sign down. She eyed him carefully. I think at first she was waiting for Dad to try and stop her, but I already knew better.

Mayor Pickens continued his fit and demanded the police arrest us all. Cullen pumped his fist from his place on the tracks of the bulldozer as the police seemed a little confused about protocol. This was Newburg, after all, Saturdays usually consisted of rescuing cats and assisting the elderly, not arresting protesters. For a moment everything went quiet, until my dad looked at my mom with nothing but love and a grin.

"You got any extra signs?"

My mom flashed a Christmas morning smile. She flung herself into Dad so hard I thought she would take him down. He wrapped his arms around her waist and they held tight. For a second or two, all was forgotten in the trampled grass and muddy tracks. Until Officer Pudgy and his buddy strolled up.

"I uh, I hate to break up this moment, but I'm going to have to ask you to leave."

It took Dad a minute to break away from Mom's gaze. He regarded the officer with a smile. "Isn't this public property, on this side at least?"

"Well, no. I mean yes, but you're interrupting the mayor's ceremony," he said, and the younger officer said something into his ear. Officer Padgett took a deep breath when Mayor Pickens, sweaty and ragged, hobbled to a wheezing halt. He looked at my dad with complete bewilderment.

"What are you doing, Ben? This is...just... You'll never work again in this town. You know that, right?"

My dad and the mayor stared each other down in the blaze of the early morning sunlight. The suits and shovels behind the mayor, the heron watching behind my dad.

"Oh, I wouldn't say that, Mr. Pickens. After all, I could always run for office."

Even the cops got a kick out of that.

27

D ad and I were parked on the couch on Friday afternoon when Mom twirled into the room and stopped directly in front of the television, holding up a couple of dresses.

"Okay, which one?"

"Mom!" I shouted. Dad and I both motioned for her to move. "The game!"

"Oh, sorry. Geez," she said, taking a step to the right. "Well?" She held up two dresses. Both looked like curtains.

The Dream Team was smashing Angola in an early qualifying round of the Olympic Games. I think the Angolan players were too starry-eyed and awestruck being on the same court with MJ, Magic, Bird, and Sir Charles to actually play real basketball.

"Definitely the blue one," Dad said, shooting me an experienced wink.

"Yeah, the blue," I deadpanned. Mom dropped both dresses to her waist. She turned to the television and gasped.

"Fifty-one to eight! This is horrible! Why are they letting them play?"

"What do you mean? It's only the first half," Dad said without taking his gaze off the television.

"The first half?" she repeated dramatically, looking back to us while pointing to the television. "But those poor players," she said, her voice getting all sappy.

"Honey, this is the Olympics, the best team wins." Dad and I high fived as Jordan hit a three-pointer.

Mom backed away, slowly starting for the hallway but unable to let it go as she left the room, mumbling, "Well, this isn't right. I don't see why they can't make it fairer."

Dad raised an eyebrow to me and we both cracked up.

While it was great spending all the extra time with Dad, the mayor's words at the ground-breaking seemed to haunt our house. Sure, he had a few leads on some jobs, but I'd overheard him griping to Mom about how no one wanted a foreman who walked away from the biggest job to ever come to Newburg. But I don't think Mom heard him, because she only stared at him all dreamy-eyed. Kind of like the Angolan players were staring at Michael Jordan.

We were front page news, again. Mom had added the clipping to our collection on the refrigerator. All of us, arms locked and shouting. After Dad and Mayor Pickens had faced off, the crowd got antsy, with Martha hopping around like a bee in a flower garden, setting her microphone under the face of anyone who would talk. Then Mitch Reynolds went postal, trashing the mayor, our town, and even Mr. Hatters who ended up shoving him to the ground. Later, as Senator Hoard slunk off, not wanting to be tangled up in such a mess, the mayor had practically gotten on his knees and begged him to stay. It was a complete mess, and the cops even had to physically remove him from the ceremony.

No ground was broken that day.

While Mom and Mr. Pickens hashed it out in the papers, Dad and I were happy to lay low as news trucks rolled through our town like Barnum and Bailey. And it wasn't just local attention anymore, because somehow the governor had caught wind of what was happening here in Newburg and stepped in. And I think that was the hardest part to believe.

Mom had pulled it off.

It all started when her column in *Newsweek* was picked up by the Associated Press. Then the *USA Today* covered the story with a picture of all of us at the ground-breaking ceremony. The one up on the fridge. Yep, little old me in the *USA Today*, I couldn't wait until Mr. Howell saw that. Can you say, extra credit?

Anyway, the next thing we knew the phone was ringing all hours and the mail started pouring in. Pretty soon, journalists, reporters, and some national environmental group traveled all the way to little Newburg, Virginia. Everyone wanted to talk to Mom.

Newsweek asked for a follow up column, a bigger piece. One Mom said might tide us over.

Seeing all the publicity she was getting, the governor called for an emergency halt to construction so an environmental action committee could look further into the situation. The governor! Mayor Pickens' shovel was still brand spanking new.

But our newfound fame wasn't all good news. In fact, Danny had called to tell me that everyone thought we were a bunch of hippie kooks. But I wasn't so worried about that anymore, not after what happened yesterday.

Cullen and I had tagged along with Mom to the grocery store, we were trying to decide between Fruity or Cocoa Pebbles when Erin Little from science class tapped me on the shoulder and smiled. I nearly collapsed into the Olympic Wheaties display, but Cullen, being so quick and smooth, caught me and smiled.

"Hey, I saw you two in the paper," Erin said, and I sort of nodded while Cullen took the lead.

"Yep, Marcus's Mom stopped the Mega More from destroying the Squabble Creek Cemetery."

"Wow." Erin smiled and again I faltered. We'd gone to

school together since the third grade but we'd never said more than a few words to each other.

"That's pretty cool," she continued. "We live down the street and my dad was worried about all the traffic."

"Oh." I rubbed my head. My hair was just starting to come in. "Well, they still might build it, it's only—Ugh!" Cullen's elbow found my ribs and shut me up quick.

"So, is this your brother?" she asked, then turned to Cullen. "How come I've never seen you at school?"

Cullen draped an arm around my neck. "Well, school isn't really my thing. And he's not my brother but my best friend."

Erin smiled and waved goodbye as she ran off to find her mom. "Okay, well I'll see you around. See you Marcus. Bye, Mystery Guy."

But even with my social life improving and being a part of the most talked about family in Newburg, I could tell by the soups and crockpot dinners and leftovers how we were scrimping. And I knew not going to work every day was killing my dad. On one hand he wasn't as worked up about deadlines and projects, but now he was moping around the house, looking for any and everything to fix. He'd made some calls, but so far, nothing was out there. I only hoped the mayor wasn't right.

But some things never changed. Sitting down to dinner, Mom passed around the crackers and then spooned out thawed out chili from winter into our bowls. Then came the first shot. "So, you know Bush doesn't stand a chance tonight, not with this format."

Dad shook his head, his eyes coming to life. "All he has to do is tell the truth. The people know who is lying."

"Can't argue that, perhaps that's why he's falling in the polls?" she said, tapping the ladle against the bowl like the opening bell to a boxing match.

And I had the best seat in the house.

I woke up on Labor Day with a sinking feeling in my gut. Like a poke or a pull, the kind I get when I know I've forgotten something but can't quite think of what it is. Mom and Dad were still asleep when I rolled out of bed, found a pair of cut-off shorts and my trusty Bulls t-shirt.

On the fridge, I studied the photo from the protest at the ground-breaking ceremony, where I stood locked to my dad on one side, Cullen on the other, my face tilted up and my mouth wide open as I sang "This Land Is Your Land." Studying the faces, I stopped at Cullen's. He was looking at me with that secret smile of his, his eyes shining even in the grainy and worn newspaper ink.

Beside it was another clipping, about the governor's halt on the construction going to the state supreme court for ruling. Dad didn't think he had the right, Mom of course backed the governor's decision. Like I said, not everything had changed in our house.

I stepped outside to get the paper. It was mild, almost chilly even. Starting for the driveway I stopped in my tracks.

My glider.

Sitting on the table in the carport, it was scratched and scraped but otherwise intact. I walked over to it and traced the wing with my finger, recognizing the stickers I'd put on crookedly in my haste to get it in the air. I picked it up and something fell off the table. When I looked down, I saw the bills and scooped them up. Seven dollars.

I ran out to the yard, gravel in the driveway biting at my bare feet as I shielded the sun with my hands, looking first to the tree, then down to Cullen's house.

The red Buick was gone, but I ran anyway, ran as fast as I could down our sleepy street to his driveway where only a patch of oil sat in its place. The ratty blue tarp lay to the side, crumpled under the weight of a few old logs and rocks. Cullen's bike wasn't laying out on the front lawn, just an indention in the tall grass.

I hopped up the front stairs, out of breath, and pounded on the door like I was going to bust it down.

I knew he was gone.

Without a goodbye or even a hint. Just my glider on the carport. I cupped my hands and looked in the window. The same tinged curtains and the same smudged walls. The same sad furniture and hopelessness where the most hopeful kid I'd ever met had lived.

Pulling my face from the window, I looked around the yard, thinking how a few weeks ago we'd cut his grass. My gaze fell to the small square of yellowed grass where some waterlogged boxes had sat, before the protest and the chanting. When my dad had a job and the summer looked to be exactly like every single one I'd ever known.

After a while I started back up to the house. The neighborhood stirred with sound. Hannibal was awake and grumbling from his window, a plane drifted past overhead, a subtle breeze tickled Mom's wind chime. I still didn't know my best friend's last name.

I did the math; he'd been there just three months. And in that time my life changed forever. He'd shown me that it was okay to be me. That it didn't matter if I was good at baseball. He taught me how to speak up for myself, that being cool was something *you* decided, not other people. But most of all, he'd taught me how to stop worrying and live.

Inside the house, Mom poured water into the coffee maker. She jumped a little as I came in and tossed the newspaper up on the counter, the headline read:

Bush Still Doesn't Get It

"So Clinton won the debate?"

Mom smiled. "Was there ever any doubt?" But when she turned around and looked at me, her smile fell. "Hey, you okay?"

I shrugged. "I think Cullen's gone."

"Gone?" She wiped her hands dry. I stared at the kitchen floor, where Cullen had slathered my legs with his homemade goop.

"Yeah, I think they're gone."

"What do you mean, 'gone'?" she said, heading for the door.

"I don't know, I just...know."

She stopped when she saw the glider I'd set on the table. Her lips parted and her expression changed, her voice whisper soft. "Your glider," she said, wrapping her arms around me.

Mom asked Dad and me to tag along for her interview at Squabble Creek. I wasn't doing much else, I'd spent most of the morning outside, hoping that maybe the Buick would return. Dad suggested packing a picnic basket. Yes, my dad. I suspected that he'd been hijacked by aliens and replaced by this impostor —this guy my mom suddenly had to hug or kiss on the cheek at least once every few minutes. It was getting to be a little much.

Pulling down the gravel road to the cemetery, it was hard to believe we were at the site of the big scene only a few weeks ago. We were a little early, so we strolled along the grounds, looking for the heron and eventually ending up at the old water mill at the bank of the creek.

It did look like a battleground. The grass was still matted and muddy from all the heavy equipment. Dad said Mega More had promised the mayor and town they weren't throwing in the towel quite yet. The chain link fence and *Keep Out* signs still stood out, not to mention the big Reynolds Construction trailer was still there. Dad never bothered to get his stuff.

Down at the creek, I climbed the boulders and skipped stones. It was cool down by the water, in the shade where the trees arched over the stream like a drawbridge. Dad pointed to a woodpecker rattling away in a tree limb overhead, and Mom nodded, her eyes faraway like she was having a conversation with nature.

When we got back to the cemetery, a shiny Jeep Cherokee was parked beside Dad's truck. Mom took a deep breath and nudged my dad. "Um, Ben, I haven't been totally honest with you."

Dad shot my mom a look. "Go on..."

"Well, my interview isn't today, and it isn't here," she said, biting her lip. "Yours is."

We stopped walking. Dad glanced up to where a man was getting out of the jeep. An older guy, with suspenders and one of those newsboy caps. He shut the door and started down toward us with a bounce in his step. I couldn't help thinking that he looked like someone who'd hang out with old Earnest Bardwell.

"His name is Clark Reston. He's with the Historical Society of Virginia. He's here to talk to you about a job."

Dad didn't have time to respond, which I guess was Mom's plan all along. Suspenders-guy ambled toward us, taking Mom in for a hug. "Well hello, Ana. It's so nice to see you," he said, and then turning to me, "And this must be Marcus."

I nodded and we shook hands, his big paw blanketed mine. "And Ben," he said, scooping his hand to Dad. Dad took it, still checking sideways at Mom who kind of shrugged with a smile. "I'm Clark Reston. It is an honor to meet you. I have to say, I've been following this story for nearly a year, and what you did was, well, remarkable to say the least."

"Well, thank you. I think, I'm not sure what to..."

"Oh," he said like he remembered something. "Please, allow me tell you why I came. When I read about you standing up to Mitch Reynolds, who, let's just say has a history of ignoring history, I called Ana and told her we might have a position for you. You see, we need someone in this area, an area of such rich tradition and history, to preserve and maintain the buildings and structures that come into our trust. And with your credentials and experience, we'd love for you to come by our offices and sit down with our people."

"Well, I uh, I must say Mr. Reston, I wasn't prepared for any of this today, but I..."

"Let me just be frank, Ben. The position is yours, if you desire," he said, his eyes drifting back to Mom. "Your character speaks for itself, and after what Ana has done..." He set an arm out toward the cemetery. "It's the least we can do."

We all looked out to the tree for a moment. Dad wasn't one for charity, but he also needed work. He agreed to meet Mr. Reston on Monday.

So Dad had a job. Mom had a job. And I was headed back to school on Monday with a summer full of memories. I ran a hand over my head. My legs were a pinkish tan and only a few dark bumps remained from the chigger bites. Pretty soon it would look like nothing had ever happened. But so much had happened.

We drove home after our picnic/job interview. Coming down our street, I craned my neck, looking for any sign of the

Buick. The driveway was still empty, and I knew it would remain empty until the next tenant moved in.

Mom drifted out to her garden. Dad dragged out the mower. I grabbed my skateboard and pushed off down the street, hopping on the board with the wind in my face. I wished Cullen could see how things were shaping up. But most of all, I hoped he knew he was my best friend, too.

I kicked hard and picked up speed. Another kick, harder than I'd ever kicked before, and harder and harder again. I was flying down the street when I came upon an arm-sized tree limb in the road. It was too late to stop and too late to swerve. Instead, I kicked the tail of the board and launched into the air, over the branch. I kept calm and stayed with the board until I came down perfectly—*slap, slap*—the back then front wheels slamming to the asphalt, my feet still on the board.

I didn't even realize what I'd done until I skidded to a stop in front of Cullen's house.

Instinctively, I glanced over to his house. Then back to my house, wondering if anyone had seen what I'd just done. My mouth hung open as I looked back to the branch in the road then to my board. Because wow, I'd done it.

"Ah snap."

Thirty Years Later

Good morning. Thank you for coming out today. This is such an exciting occasion for me on both a personal and professional level. As I look out over this great, vast land, I'm humbled by the tranquil beauty of Mother Nature. And I think in this world of technology and screen time, a little tranquility is a great thing.

As your mayor, I urge you to do the same. Take a moment to look around and appreciate the natural beauty behind me. Please, go ahead, it's much more interesting than a bunch of old guys talking to you from a podium.

Look to the chestnut tree, where you might see a blue heron perched on the limb, ready to take a dip in the creek. Thirty years ago, those herons were nearly extinct. But today they are flourishing.

Past the tree, you will find the cemetery, honoring those mistreated, fallen in war, those who stood to protect our country and keep it intact.

On the creek bank, you may find the remains of the old water mill, once a vital part of life near our water source. Or you may just like to listen, as I do on occasion, when I'm not up here blathering.

To the students in attendance, I'd like to take a moment to address you directly. Don't worry, you can keep looking for the heron, I don't mind.

Not so long ago, I stood in this field, listening to a mayor speak not far from where I'm speaking today. I had no idea of the power my voice had then, that standing up for what is right, against the odds, can be the difference. But it was the difference. I saw it happen. I saw first-hand what can happen when people stand up and get involved. I saw how one woman could take on a giant.

And win.

As a human I want to leave this earth better than I found it. In my lifetime, I've seen Wilson Road and the town of Newburg grow and progress. With its shops and stores, and ever-expanding lanes, there's no doubt Newburg has prospered. But when I look around here today, I see how Squabble Creek has prospered, too.

And now, as we gather here today to unveil the historical site marker, I am filled with pride to be affiliated with this great town.

So many people have made this day possible, but none more than my own mother, Ana Hawthorne. She's here in attendance today. I have my mother to thank—or blame—for getting involved in politics. I watched her fight tooth and nail, against all odds, to keep Squabble Creek the sanctuary it still is today. My mother taught me to listen to the call of nature. She instilled a sense of urgency to protect and respect nature. As a son, I strive to make my parents proud. Because I learned through their actions what it means to do the right thing.

I'd also like to extend thanks to the Historical Society of Virginia. The beautiful chapel in the cemetery has been restored to its former glory. I'd like to offer my gratitude to all the private donors. Through their efforts and the volunteer work and fund raising, the cemetery has been preserved, cleaned, and cleared so that the families of those resting can find their loved ones. And finally, thanks to the fine folks at Mega More, we can look to the awareness gardens and reflect on our past and the present. They have been a terrific partner in this endeavor.

I believe community and business can prosper together. As Newburg continues to grow, it will do so as a community, partnering with both corporations and small businesses. I believe in finding a cooperative way to work together, and that with prosperity comes a civic duty to give back to our community.

Just as my mother made peace with Mega More, I hope Newburg has made peace with Squabble Creek. The landscape that remains intact today is due to the tireless efforts of those who chose to stand up and protect it. And now, with the resources provided by local businesses and private donations alike, I believe it is up to all of us to continue to protect it for generations to come.

Thank you.

Mayor Marcus K. Hawthorne

LOOKING FOR MORE?

Read on for an exclusive look at Fanning's novel, *The Thing About Dad* (January 2022, Immortal Works).

THE THING ABOUT DAD -
CHAPTER 1

Somewhere in Virginia our two-day, five-state journey came to a weary stop in the driveway of a strange house. I looked through a smear of mangled wings and bug guts on the windshield, to a weeping willow tree sagging in the heat. Its wilted leaves seemed to be begging for a breeze.

"Well?" Dad said, waiting for my reaction as the car ticked and hissed. My gaze followed the brick walkway to the porch where the ferns spilled from hanging baskets, as though searching for water between the large white columns.

"This is it?" I asked, a glint of hope catching my voice.

Hot as it was, I had to admit, the house was cool. Dad called it a bungalow, but to me, with its big green shutters and the upstairs window jutting right out onto the roof, it looked like a big clubhouse.

Dad threw his hands up. "This is it."

Untangling my feet from the nest of candy wrappers, potato chip bags, and soda bottles, I crawled out of the car, shaking my legs to life as we climbed the steps. Dad watched me closely, still trying to sell me on this little adventure, like he had been since the day he came home and announced his big promotion.

Wasn't happening. There was nothing he could say to make me like Virginia. I was thirteen and would have to start over at some random middle school, having ditched my old friends and abandoned my spot as co-captain of the hockey team. He was the parent and I was the hostage.

Promotion. More like a *demotion*. Like I wanted to be here, choking down thick, muggy air in mid-July on the porch of some strange house—even if it did have a porch swing I was dying to test out.

Dad hung an arm around my shoulder. *Here comes the sales pitch,* I thought. "Look, I'm nervous too. I've lived in North Country my whole life, just like you. But sometimes life hurls opportunities at us, and we have to take chances."

I glanced up to my captor, his stormy blue eyes upbeat and hopeful. He was good with the pep talks, I'd give him that. Otherwise I wouldn't have gotten in the car. I'd still be in Grandpa's house, sipping a frosty Coke and watching the Rangers' game on his old floor model television. I dropped my eyes, not wanting to have the same tired conversation again.

Dad took the hint, sliding his arm off me and then slapping the beam above our heads with a stretch. "The movers should be here soon," he said with a nudge. "Come on, I'll give you a quick tour."

The house was stifling hot. Dad scampered to the living room and adjusted the thermostat, and the vents rattled to life.

"Please tell me that's air conditioning," I said, running my hand along the stone fireplace. I'd never lived in a house with air conditioning. Never needed to until now.

The sun streamed through two small windows on either side of the fireplace, bouncing off the polished floors. It smelled like new paint on the walls. Again, the place was sweet, but I was holding out because I hadn't seen my room yet.

An archway led to the kitchen, then out to a large wooden

deck facing a wall of trees. "Okay," Dad said, rubbing his hands together dramatically. "Time for the moment of truth."

I followed him up the stairs where, even if the house was actually on fire it couldn't have been much hotter. Dad motioned to the rooms. "You're on the right, I'm on the left. The bathroom is straight ahead."

I hung a right and opened the door, wiping sweat from my forehead. Wow, okay. My room was huge, way bigger than home. More new smells encircled me, of cedar and floor polish. The ceilings sloped downwards to the large window overlooking the neighborhood. I looked out to the street where a kid putted around the curb on his bike. When he glanced up I eased back.

Dad's room was even bigger than mine, and he had his own door to the bathroom. The perks of paying rent, I guessed. Bending down, I held my face over the vents to make sure cool air was blowing. Dad chuckled. "It works, Jack."

"Just testing," I said, standing and relishing the icy blast up my shorts. "So how do you think Grandpa's doing?"

"I'm sure he's fine. Probably enjoying the peace and quiet without you banging on the drums," he said with a smile. Dad had jokes.

We'd checked in with Papa last night from the hotel, but still, it was hard leaving him back in upstate New York. It had always been just the three of us, and I liked it that way. Where Dad was laid back, Grandpa was tough as rust. He'd fought in Vietnam and had all sorts of medals and pictures and even his uniform. But Grandpa wasn't *all* tough guy, he could be cool— his jokes were epic. Dad said he'd softened up over the years, since Grandma passed. I wondered if the same thing happened to Dad after Mom died.

Some rumbling outside. The sneeze of air brakes. I ran for the window. "They're here!"

We rushed downstairs and out to the porch. The moving

truck jerked and jostled as it hopped the curb, backing onto the grass and lurching for the steps. Dad jumped down and helped guide the truck in after the driver nearly took out a row of boxwoods. Finally, we waved him to a halt.

The doors creaked open and two of the oldest movers alive hobbled out of the truck. "How ya'll doing?" The driver croaked, wiping his brow with a bandanna. I snorted at his drawl. Dad cut his eyes my way. He'd said his company was paying for the move and these guys came with the deal.

When the back door slid up, it looked like the truck had rolled over twice and then flipped once more to be sure everything was overturned and collapsed. My stomach twisted, because my drum set—my most cherished possession in the world—was somewhere in the midst of the wreckage.

One of the movers, Harry or Larry (I could only make out the *arry*), whistled low and then muttered something I couldn't understand. Dad shrugged, and we began sorting through the mess.

Thankfully, most of the fallen boxes were Dad's books. Not sure why the geniuses set the books on top of everything, but then again I'm not a professional mover. We dug in, got my bed upstairs, then my desk—the bottom of which still had a few *Monsters Inc.* stickers stuck to it from forever ago. And finally, in the back, safe and sound and thankfully unblemished, we found my kit, the one thing I could not live without.

Out in the yard I inspected each piece for damage. Dad knelt beside me, wiping his brow with a towel. Everyone was soaked with sweat.

"How's it look? Everything okay?"

I nodded. "I think so."

"Nice. Hey, looks like we have company."

I looked up to find the kid I'd seen out the window shuffling over. He wore a hat that was way too big for his head, crooked glasses, and his stick legs sprouted out of loose socks and untied high-top sneakers.

"Is that a drum set?"

"Um, yeah," I said with a smirk, looking over my kick drum. The chrome of my snare drum sparkled in the bright sunshine.

"Cool," the kid said. He fixed his hat and sat down. I looked over to him and he smiled. "I'm Trevor Walker." His freckles bounced when he spoke.

"I'm Jack. Dufresne."

He hovered over me for a while, firing off question after question, clapping his hands in front of his face to bat away the swarms of gnats. *So, you play the drums? What grade are you in? Are ya'll moving in?*

"Yeah, me and my dad," I said to his last question with a laugh. He laughed too.

"Cool."

With my drums safe, I helped Dad haul in some chairs. Trevor, my new shadow, tagged along at my hip. But it was kind of nice to have some company after being stuck in the car for the past few days, and besides, listening to him babble gave me something to do other than grumble to Dad about the heat.

Late afternoon, Trevor's parents arrived to welcome us. Trevor's mom went through the introductions—Mr. Walker was a dentist, and she was a teacher. They lived at the bottom of the street and loved the neighborhood, blah blah blah, something about their daughter at a friend's house.

They seemed okay. They didn't stay long, dragging Trevor away and letting us get back to work after the movers dropped something in the other room. On their way out, Mrs. Walker offered dinner again, but Dad assured them we'd be fine—which meant we were ordering pizza.

After they left, we cranked up the tunes. My dad is forty but he plays guitar and likes to hang out. Sure, he can be strict and stern and all parental and stuff, but he's a kid at heart and pretty easy to read.

At some point I got stuck with taking junk down to the basement. At the bottom of the steps, I dropped a box of books and yanked on the overhead pull strings until I found a light that worked. The basement was unfinished, with cinderblock walls and pipes and wires running along the ceiling. In other words, it was the perfect spot to jam. Near the back, I found a storage room with some old dusty furniture and shelves filled with nuts and bolts that jingled when Harry or Larry stomped down the steps, piled some wrinkled boxes in the corner with a grunt, then marched back upstairs, shutting the door behind him and leaving me alone with the plodding footsteps and muffled voices over my head.

It was nice and cool down there, and one of those boxes contained the hockey cards Grandpa had given me just before we left. It was his *The Miracle on Ice* set and he'd said it was worth a little bit of money. Dad and I hadn't exactly labeled the boxes, so I just ripped into the one on top. Board games. Great. I moaned at the thought of the two of us sitting around playing Scrabble on a Saturday night, an ancient dictionary cracked open as we argued over my use of a slang.

I set the games aside and tore into box number two—a bunch of old spiral bound composition books like you'd get for school. Only there were maybe twenty of them. I ran my finger along the metal binds, then for some reason, picked one out.

On the first splotchy yellow page I saw my mom's name, *Ellie*, then my name. It was a journal or something. I swallowing a big, musty gulp of basement air and fell against the cool cinderblock wall, flipping through the pages, catching little bits and pieces.

I had a dream about you last night...

Flip.

Jack had his first recital at school...

Flip.

Life isn't the same without you...

I shut the book and clutched it to my chest. What in the world? Of all the stuff my dad and I talked about—music, sports, school—Ellie, my mom, was not on the list. I wouldn't even know where to begin. It was why what I was holding—written proof she had been a real person and not just some smile in a frame—felt like a long lost treasure map.

My heart galloped. I slid down to the floor, a shiver rippling through my skin as I flipped back to the first page.

Dear Ellie,

The upstairs door swung open and I scrambled to my feet, kicking over the pile of board games and sending dice and cards and Monopoly money across the floor. I fumbled my way back toward the boxes when Dad called down, "Jack?"

I stuffed the notebook back with the others, glanced at the mess on the floor, and then bounded up the stairs full stride.

Dad gave me a once over. "You okay?"

"Yeah, I'm okay," I said, a little out of breath and lightheaded from the stairs or the box or just, everything. I tried to meet his gaze but looked away, back toward the steps, unable to come up with anything to say. Thankfully, Tom Petty blared off the empty walls, his familiar voice making things almost normal again.

Dad patted me on the shoulder and said something about going to find the towels.

Life in Virginia was off to a very weird start.

Author's Note

My house was always lively growing up. Be it dinner, game night, during a commercial break between shows, my dad and stepmom would often discuss world events. If Crossfire was on, it usually led to the two of them duking it out, with my dad out of his seat, pacing, his arms flying as he made his point about an issue he believed in. When the pacing stopped and he stood heaving, my stepmom would gently set her paperback on her lap, try and fail to hide her smirk, before calmly countering each and every point he'd made.

I would watch like a tennis match. This, I learned quickly, was politics. My parents rarely saw things eye to eye back then, but for me it was like a history lesson, civics class, and debate club all in one. They spanned the globe, from Watergate to the Berlin Wall, World Wars to Reaganomics, my parents would hash it out then kiss and make up. It was weird, gross, and completely fascinating all at once.

Acknowledgments

Thanks to the usual suspects. To the Immortal Works crew. To Staci Olsen for bringing me in. To my favorite editor, Holli Anderson for cleaning things up.

Thanks to Diane Fanning for the inspiration. To Dad, for being the greatest. Thanks to Nana, my favorite beta reader. To John and Jocelyne Lavigne. To Simon, the coolest kid I know. To Bella, our jokester. Most of all, thanks to my wife, Anne, who may not always know the answer but always wins the debates!

About the Author

Pete Fanning is the author of *Justice in a Bottle* and *Runaway Blues*. He lives in Virginia with his wife, son, baby girl, and two very spoiled dogs. He can be found at www.petefanning.com, where he's posted over 200 flash fiction stories.

This has been an
Immortal Production